CHESHIRE IN HEARTSLAND

A WONDERLAND EVER AFTER NOVEL

ARIELLA ZOELLE

Cover Design by Natasha of Natasha Snow Designs

Editing by Pam of Undivided Editing

Proofreading by Sandra of One Love Editing

ISBN: 978-1-954202-18-4

DEDICATION

For those who dreamed of living in a Wonderland with a talking Cheshire cat.

" I f you weren't so stubborn, I could pleasure you instead of using your hand," I said from the shadows.

King Rei of Hearts sat up with an undignified swear over being caught touching himself. "Cheshire!"

I emerged from my hiding place, sauntering over to the bed with a cocky smirk. "At your service," I purred as I crawled toward him on all fours, pinning him down. "All you have to do is say the word."

He glared up at me with those fierce red eyes I loved so much. "Give me one reason not to call the guards in here."

"I doubt you'll want them to see His Royal Majesty at full attention." Although I was in my human form, my cat tail brushed against his erection. He inhaled sharply as he tensed under me. "Besides, we both know that's an empty threat when there isn't a dungeon anywhere in the kingdom that could trap a shifter as magical as me."

"I'm in no mood for your games tonight."

"Let me take care of you like I used to," I pleaded, stroking his prick with my tail in a silent bid for reconsideration. We had been lovers before he had become king three years ago and decided he wasn't allowed to have fun or openly love me anymore. "I can make us both feel better."

"What would make me feel better is if you'd leave me alone."

It was the same claim he always fell back on when he was losing the fight against his desire for me. "We both know that's a lie, so why do you keep saying it like it's true?"

For once, he didn't argue with me. "You can't be here."

"Because Prince Renner arrives tomorrow for his marriage interview with you?" I narrowed my eyes in displeasure, rankling at Rei's responsibilities as king forcing him into such an unsavory situation.

The regret on his face mollified me somewhat.

"You know I didn't want to agree to that, but I had no choice."

"Wrong. You could choose to be with me instead," I insisted. "Now that the magic has returned to Wonderland and the shifters have reemerged from their long hibernation, there's no reason for you to keep rejecting me."

"That doesn't mean my people will accept you as my royal consort." Rei sighed with old frustrations. "Your reputation as a troublemaker and hell-raiser—"

"If you were mine again, I'd be as docile as a dormouse," I promised with a pleading gaze. "I wouldn't need to cause any trouble when I'd finally have everything I want."

It surprised me when he pulled me down into an embrace. "Please don't look at me like that. It makes it too difficult to tell you no, Chess."

Despite my displeasure, I delighted in the small show of affection. I nuzzled against him with a purr, even as his still-hard prick made me want to do more than waste time talking. "Give me the chance to charm your people and reassure their fears about me. I promise you they like me far more than you think they do. I don't know why you believe the townsfolk aren't fans."

He hugged me tighter. "I wish it was that easy."

"At least let me try before I lose you for good." I rocked against his hardness, earning me a sharp breath. "Please, Rei."

He guided me to look down at him. "I can't get out of the marriage interview, but you have my word I won't fall for Prince Renner."

I pouted. "But everyone says he's Prince Charming, a perfect blend of gorgeous, generous, and kind. He's everything a king's consort should be. It would be the height of foolishness not to choose him to stand by your side."

Rei ran his fingers through my hair as I nuzzled against his palm. "When I became king, I vowed if I can't be with you, then I'll be with no one. I have no intention of breaking my word."

His words should have made me feel better, but they didn't. I hated that he stubbornly chose to be alone when he didn't have to. "Why would your people want to be ruled by a King of Hearts who can't love?"

"It's not that I can't love. It's that I can't love you openly. There's a difference."

"You beautiful, stupid, stubborn man." I'd had enough of his words that tugged at my heartstrings and made us both sad. Instead of arguing, I gave in to the forbidden urge I had resisted since the eve of King Rei's coronation. I kissed him with all the pent-up love that I had been forced to hold back for the past three years of his reign.

Rather than pushing me away as I had expected, Rei's hands tugged me down as he kissed me back with a burning need that fueled my fire. It made me greedy as I demanded entrance to his mouth, claiming it as mine once more. I used my magic to get rid of my clothes, allowing me to brush my arousal against his, with nothing between us.

He gasped as his body stiffened with the shock of sudden skin-to-skin contact. But I didn't relent as I drowned in the taste of him I had missed so much. It drove my beast wild when Rei rocked his hardness against mine as his nails scratched against my scalp.

Since he hadn't stopped me, I continued to push the boundaries of his tolerance. I took both of our arousals in hand and used my magic to slick them.

"We can't!" Rei gasped.

"We can, and we are." I pumped our lengths with a firm grip, earning me the most beautiful gasps from my beloved as he writhed under me. "We've waited long enough."

It gratified my ego that his protests stopped as he continued kissing me. Now that we had finally given in to our lust after three years of teasing, nothing could stop us as we raced to our climaxes. I nipped at his lips with my fang teeth since that had always spiked his enjoyment in the past. He thrust into my hand with more urgency as his tongue got reacquainted with the sharp points of them.

"We shouldn't do this," he whispered against my neck as he buried his face there with a moan.

"Do you really want me to stop?"

His answer stunned me. "*No.*"

I redoubled my efforts as my hand picked up the pace. While I hadn't claimed Rei as my fated mate with a mating bond yet, it was still my duty to tend to his every need. And I wasn't stopping until our seed decorated his skin with the evidence of our love that had languished for far too long because of his stubbornness and old fears.

CHAPTER

TWO

REI

If I was kissing Cheshire, I couldn't do something stupid like tell him to stop. As long as his tongue tangoed with mine, it kept me from sobbing with relief at *finally* having him take care of my needs again. When he teased me with his fangs, I couldn't list all the reasons I owed it to my kingdom not to give in to our lust. While he worked my arousal, I could pretend I was only his Rei and not the lonely King of Hearts.

After three years of my hand being my sole comfort and companion during my lonely nights, having Cheshire take control of my desires was the best kind of heaven. I yearned to have him moving inside me again, but even in my euphoric state, I knew that was a bridge we couldn't cross. It would already be hard enough telling him no after tonight. But if I gave myself to him, the word "no" would cease to exist. However, I refused to be as selfish as my tyrannical mother, the former Queen of Hearts. I had to deny him in order to continue my reign.

"Stay with me, Rei," Cheshire implored me, brushing his thumb over the tip of my prick to refocus me. "Focus on how good this feels."

Instead of the painful barbed spines on the base of a regular cat's penis, Cheshire always softened them to small bumps that gave the most exquisite friction. It was another part of his feline heritage that secretly drove me wild from how different it was from my anatomy and how amazing it felt to have that slight hint of texture rubbing against me.

I had already ruined three years of resistance by giving in, so I owed it to myself to enjoy the experience that could never be repeated. My body tensed as I raced toward my peak faster than I wanted. But after suffering without his touch for so long, it was impossible not to lose myself to the overwhelming pleasure. "Please, Chess. I need—"

"I've got you, my love. I know exactly what you need." He proved it by using his magic to penetrate me, letting it expand in my tight channel and move in sync with his hand, flooding me with heat. I arched up under him with a moan, somehow satisfied and still craving more.

I didn't want the moment to be over, but when his powers swirled against that spot inside me that Cheshire was so good at manipulating, I came with a soft cry of his name I couldn't smother. It resulted in him orgasming, making a spectacular mess on my stomach when combined with my release.

That should have been the end, but I wasn't ready for it to be over yet. I tugged him down for a desperate kiss, silently begging him to stay with me before I had to ruin everything for the sake of my kingdom.

He indulged me before he began trailing kisses down my neck and chest. My breathing hitched when I realized what he was intending to do. He lapped at our seed mixed together on my stomach, making me moan when he impishly added the little spines on his cat tongue to tease me. The rough drag against my skin gave me a shameful pleasure that I was too blissed out to resist.

Instead of telling him to stop, I ran my fingers through his long, purple-and-fuchsia hair, then stroked his soft ears while he lapped up our cum. He leaned into the caress with a purr of contentment.

How long had it been since I had earned the privilege of making him purr?

His amber eyes glowed with the unnatural light of his inner beast for a moment before returning to normal. "I've missed the sweet taste of your pleasure," he rumbled, sending shivers of lust through me as he continued cleaning me. "Almost as much as I missed being inside you and hearing you moan so beautifully." His fingers strayed down to rim around my hole, making my breath catch.

I subtly shifted away from his touch. "We've already done too much as it is."

He moved his hand away. I was about to sigh in relief when he extended his nails into claws to caress my side while he took his time licking me clean. It drew an unintentional whimper from me as I ached for him to touch me all over with those claws that drove me to madness.

"Does this mean you've come to your senses?" Cheshire asked.

"This doesn't change the fact that I still have to meet Prince Renner tomorrow for our marriage interview." Saying the words out loud was a knife to the heart.

For once, Cheshire didn't react. He continued grooming me until he licked off the last splatter of cum. Only then did he sprawl on top of me like the indulgent cat he was. "What if he doesn't make it to the palace?"

The question filled me with dread, even as I wrapped my arms around him. "You can't harm him when he is under my care from the moment he steps foot on my land. It will reflect badly on me and do nothing to endear you to my people."

"Who said anything about harming him?" Cheshire used his claws to tease my nipple into a hardened peak. "But perhaps he asks at a crossroads whether he should go hither or thither and receives a wrong answer from a mad cat?"

"The sooner he arrives, the sooner he can leave. Don't prolong our misery by making him stay longer because of misdirection."

I could hear the pout in Cheshire's voice. "But the little princeling deserves it for trying to come here and steal what's rightfully mine."

"He's probably as disinterested in me as I am in him. But just like me, he's obligated to do this because of his role." I couldn't imagine why a young royal would be interested in someone as notoriously grumpy as me. "Promise me you won't cause problems."

"Swear this wasn't a onetime occurrence, and I'll consider it."

"You know this can't happen again." I tried to ignore the painful tugging on my heart at the thought of denying myself the pleasure of being with the only person I had ever loved. "My people would rise in rebellion."

"I can live with being the royal secret, as long as I can be with you alone in private." He kissed my chest before nuzzling me. "I don't need the whole world to know you're in love with me. I just need you, Rei."

And I needed him more than the air I breathed. But how could we ever be together in a world that demanded we stay apart?

I t wasn't hard to find Prince Renner in the forest. His carriage was covered in the mirrors that represented his homeland. They cast prisms of rainbows everywhere, making quite a spectacle in the woods.

I bided my time until they stopped to give the horses some rest. Prince Renner got out of the carriage, giving me my first proper glimpse of him. He was tall, lithe, and had beautiful seafoam-green hair with blue highlights that cascaded around him in gentle waves. His eyes were a similar enchanting shade of sea glass, giving him an ethereal beauty that was sure to make all the aristocrats at court swoon over him once he arrived at the palace.

I watched from my invisible vantage point as he

instructed his guards to lead the horses to water. He followed behind them at a much more leisurely pace as he marveled at his surroundings like a royal who didn't get out in the wild very often. In his iridescent teal tunic and white britches, he was the vision of a fairy-tale prince who would be a perfect consort to the king. Worse, he looked like someone my mate could easily learn to love.

That simply wouldn't do. Rather than becoming maudlin, it was time to act. I used my invisibility to my advantage, rustling the leaves in the trees above him suspiciously. "You look lost, little princeling," I said in an echoing voice that made it impossible to tell which direction it came from originally.

Rather than freezing with panic, his beautiful eyes lit up with delight. "Are you the infamous Cheshire cat?" Prince Renner asked, his tone laced with excitement as he looked around the area.

That generally wasn't the reaction most people had to me. Clearly, the little princeling was too naïve to know better.

I lounged on a tree branch with one paw dangling down as I slowly revealed myself from my tail to the tips of my ears. "Indeed, it is I, the master of mischief and mayhem."

To my surprise, he clasped his hands together as

he gazed up at me with awe. "It's really you! Oh, how marvelous! It truly must be my lucky day."

I tilted my head as I regarded him. "Why do you not fear me as most do?"

"Because I think you're the most amazing creature in all of Wonderland." There was genuine admiration in his voice as he stared at me. "I agreed to come here because I was hoping I'd be fortunate enough to meet you."

I swished my tail in annoyance that the encounter wasn't going according to plan. "Are you saying you came to meet me and not King Rei?"

"I have to meet him, but I wanted to meet you," Prince Renner said with an earnestness that made it very hard to stay cross with him. "Your exploits are legendary. I love how you give hell to all those stuffy aristocrats I can't stand." He crinkled his nose adorably.

"You're a fan because I cause trouble for people like you?" I rested my chin on my paws. "Perhaps you are more mad than me."

"I'd give up being a royal in a heartbeat if it meant I got to live a life of love and adventure." The wistfulness in his voice tugged on my heartstrings. "As the sixth son and twelfth child, I'm just a pawn for my parents. I'd rather run away from it all and fall in love for real than have to suffer through an arranged marriage."

While I wholeheartedly approved of his desire to escape his awful lot in life, part of me was still offended. "You should be more grateful. You would be lucky to marry someone as amazing as King Rei."

Prince Renner studied me for a long moment before he said something so shocking I almost fell out of the tree. "But you're in love with him, aren't you?"

I flicked my tail with irritation. "And what would you know of such things, young princeling?"

"I've heard people whisper that the two of you are lovers."

"People say many things, but it doesn't make rumors true." I gave a disdainful sniff for good measure.

Prince Renner was about to say something when one of his guards called out to him. With surprising alacrity, he climbed the tree to sit on the branch with me. He put his finger to his lips when his guard walked by in search of him.

I gave him the courtesy of obeying, but only because I burned with a need to know what he intended to say.

Once the threat of discovery passed, he shifted to lean back against the tree and look at me. "So, is what they say true? Are you and the king in love?" Prince Renner asked in a hushed voice.

Rather than demurring on the subject, I staked my claim on my mate. "We are, but Rei's fear of his people rejecting me stops us from being together."

"Oh, that simply won't do. We must find a way to change his mind."

I blinked in disbelief. Surely, I must have heard wrong? "*We?*"

"Life is too short not to be with the person you love." He beseeched me with those beautiful eyes that were the color of where the sea met the sky. "Please do me the honor of letting me help you."

"Why in the world would you want to do that?" His sincere desire baffled me.

"Because you deserve to be with the man you love, and getting to help someone I admire so much find his happiness would be amazing." His smile turned impish. "It also would anger that awful diplomat Marram who arranged this marriage interview, which is a lovely little bonus. Ruining her plans is so much more fun than being an obedient puppet who does what she wants."

"Perhaps we are kindred spirits, after all." My opinion of Prince Renner went up quite a few notches. "You truly wish to help me make King Rei my mate, even though you'll find yourself in a great deal of trouble back at home?"

"*Especially* because I'll get into trouble for it." He grinned at me. "That's what will make it so much fun!"

"Very well, Prince Renner of Mirrorland. I shall allow you to help me win over my stubborn beloved." To seal the deal, I held out my paw to him.

He shook it with as much seriousness as if it was my human hand. "We'll make sure true love wins. What do you say to riding with me in the carriage and making our plans on the way to the palace?"

"That sounds like a wise use of time." Rei was going to be *so* annoyed that I had swayed the prince to my side. That made our scheme even more delightful.

"Prince Renner!" As his exasperated guard appeared, I realized that it was Tweedledee, who I hadn't seen in many long years. That meant Tweedledum must have been with the horses. "Where have you run off to?"

The young royal waited until the man passed by us to drop behind him. Tweedledee's startled reaction as he fell down with surprise made me snicker from my place in the tree.

"I'm right here," Prince Renner said brightly. "Let's get on our way, shall we?"

Tweedledee stood up, brushing the leaves off his silver uniform. "As you wish, Your Highness."

They began walking in the road's direction. I had to grin when Prince Renner silently signaled me from behind to join him. How unexpected to find out he was a fan of mine because I liked to cause troubles for royals.

I followed him into the carriage, which had seats made of an iridescent purple fabric with gold paint on the walls.

"Cheshire, are you here?" Prince Renner asked under his breath as the carriage moved.

I revealed myself in my human form, reveling in his star-struck expression. "Indeed, I am."

"Wow, it's no wonder you're a cat most of the time. When you're that handsome, you'd have people falling all over themselves to be with you if you walked around like that." There was a charming hint of a blush on his cheeks.

I chuckled at his claim. "It's kind of you to say, but my reputation precedes me. A beautiful visage does not undo centuries of being a meddlesome cat."

"I'm curious. Which do you think is more likely to

work: me pretending to flirt with King Rei or me acting like I have a romantic crush on you?"

I stroked my chin as I mulled over the options. "Rei would begrudgingly put up with your amorous advances as part of his royal duties. But pretending you want me is something he'd be wholly unprepared for." The more I thought about it, the more I liked the idea. "I daresay it might draw out his jealous side because he's never had a reason to think I'd be with anyone other than him."

"Which would mean he'd probably feel the need to claim you before I stole you away from him, right?"

I gave the young royal an appraising gaze. It seemed there was more to him than met the eye. "That would be the ideal reaction." I grinned as I imagined scenarios in my head. "He's expecting me to dissuade you from being interested in him. To discover I've been charmed by you would be most unsettling to him."

"I can start off by subtly asking questions about you."

"Subtle isn't my style." I smirked as an idea came to mind. "No, I think me accompanying you at your first meeting will be much more fun."

Prince Renner grinned. "And by fun, you mean cause chaos, right?"

"Of course. It's the thing I'm the very best at." I could have purred with delight at the unexpected turn of events. Catching Rei off guard would be even more fun than my original plan to chase off the young royal.

P rince Renner appeared with a flourish of fanfare, flanked by identical twin guards. He was as handsome as the rumors suggested, with seafoam-green hair that had intricate braids which enhanced his almost elven appearance. His smile was friendly and kind, while I was trying my hardest not to scowl in annoyance at the beautiful ray of sunshine that was approaching my throne.

"May I introduce Prince Renner of the royal house of Mirrorland, the sixth son of our honorable King Otto and Queen Emme," a stodgy male diplomat announced. Nayan was humorless and dull but a welcomed change over that awful Marram who had forced the marriage interview. The imminent arrival of her first grandchild had spared me that misfortune.

Prince Renner bowed as he stood before me, gazing up at me with an openness I wasn't used to seeing in other royals. "It is a great pleasure to make your acquaintance, Your Majesty."

While I wasn't interested in the prince, I still owed him my polite manners. After all, it wasn't his fault he was being used as a pawn by his parents. "Thank you for enduring a long journey to visit my kingdom. I hope it wasn't too arduous."

"Oh, it was tremendous fun!" He radiated joy in a way that made me nostalgic for my own carefree days, when I had loved Cheshire freely without worrying about any royal duties. "I've always dreamed of coming here, so it was an honor to be invited by you."

There was something so genuine about him that it baffled me. "Why did you wish to come here?"

"Because this is where all the shifters lived and the lands that Alice once roamed. Your Alistair restoring magic to all of Wonderland renewed my interest in a visit."

I arched an eyebrow at him. "You don't fear shifters?"

"Quite the opposite. I find them such fascinating creatures, more so than any Jabberwocky or griffin."

"That's unusual for someone of your age." I winced at how old the comment made me sound, although the difference between us was not that great. "Even now that they have returned, many still fear them and their abilities."

His expression turned sympathetic. "It will take time for them to unlearn their old superstitions. But I hope everyone will grow fond of them now that they've returned."

"Your optimism is to be commended." I wasn't as certain that the people in my kingdom would embrace shifters the way I would need them to if I were ever to be with Cheshire.

His lips turned up in an amused grin. "You don't seem to share my positive outlook on the situation."

"I have seen the distrust firsthand. That is a prejudice that may take centuries to unlearn."

His sea-glass-colored eyes studied me with curiosity. "Do you think it's all shifters or just the Cheshire cat the people fear?"

It seemed the young prince was more astute than I gave him credit for. I'd have to be careful. Rather than answering, I dodged the question. "And what do you know of the Cheshire cat?"

Prince Renner's expression lit up with joy. "He's the most marvelous shifter in all of Wonderland!"

I was unprepared for his unabashed enthusiasm for my former lover. "Many do not share your viewpoint. Most consider him a menace."

"Then they are small-minded and fearful of what they cannot understand." He gave a dismissive wave of his hand. "Anyone who has heard the legends should admire Cheshire and his incredible power. It's been my dream to meet him."

I glanced around the room, expecting the prince's words to summon the troublesome cat who loved attention. But he was suspiciously absent, which didn't sit well with me at all. "Should you make his acquaintance, he will surely puff up with pride at hearing that."

Prince Renner clasped his hands together as he looked up at me hopefully. "Would it be too forward to ask if you could arrange a meeting with him? After all, you're great friends with him."

My need to be an excellent host warred with my desire to keep the two men as far apart as possible. No good could come of Cheshire meeting the young royal. When the cat shifter resented the prince's arrival, there was no telling what mischief he would cause. "Is that what the rumors say?"

A faint blush graced his cheeks. "Some of them. Others say you're far closer than mere friends."

His words unsettled me. "That doesn't make their idle chatter true." The expectant look in his eyes made me inwardly sigh. "Unfortunately, Cheshire is a cat who does as he pleases. He does not respond well to orders from anyone, not even from his king."

"That's not true," Cheshire's voice said. He slowly appeared in his cat form, starting from the tip of his tail to the ends of his whiskers. "I'm always pleased to do what you ask when it's something I want to do."

I clamped down on my urge to reprimand him for appearing in the palace without permission. No matter how many times I reminded him that he was banned, he showed a flagrant disregard for that fact. I also ignored the very un-kinglike panic I felt over his sudden appearance.

Prince Renner looked at Cheshire with open admiration. "It really is you!"

Cheshire shifted into his human form, although he kept his cat ears and tail. He was extra handsome in his violet jacquard suit designed by Hatter. It took an effort not to react when he reached out to take the prince's hand and bring it up to his lips to kiss while looking deep into his eyes. "What a treat it is to meet a fan." He glanced at me over his shoulder. "*Someone* could stand to learn a thing or two about giving a warm welcome."

I bristled at the dig but knew it was smarter to keep my silence. Losing my cool would make me look terrible in front of my guest. I wasn't interested in taking him as my consort, but I owed it to myself to maintain my dignity as a ruler.

Prince Renner clasped Cheshire's hand in his as he looked at him with a loving adoration that made me uncomfortable. "I can't believe my good fortune! I've longed to meet you since I was a child, and you're right here in front of me, even more magnificent than the rumors said."

Jealousy burned deep within me. It filled me with an urge to lay claim to Cheshire in a way that would leave no doubt in anyone's mind that he was *mine*. But I couldn't do that, although there was nothing I wanted more than to live a quiet life with him.

"What a charming young princeling you are," Cheshire purred, clearly loving the attention. "How unexpected."

I clenched my hands into tight fists before I forced myself to relax. If he realized how much the interaction bothered me, it would only encourage him to flirt more. But I had to separate the two of them before I lost my mind to jealousy.

CHAPTER
FIVE
CHESHIRE

My ego purred at watching Rei struggle with me turning on the charm instead of lashing out at the young prince as I had first planned. It encouraged me to continue pushing the boundaries of the king's tolerance.

I stroked under Renner's chin as I forced him to look up to hold my gaze. "Perhaps I should steal you for myself," I said, although I had no interest in doing so. "That would be a magic trick worthy of a grand Cheshire cat such as myself."

"You will leave him alone," Rei said in a voice that was filled with more ice than the Wibbly Bibbly Lake in the dead of winter.

I turned to face him, unable to resist pushing him

for a reaction. "Are you saying that because you want him all to yourself? Or is it me you desire?"

The fire burning in Rei's ruby-red eyes filled me with an unbearable heat. It urged me to do things that would almost certainly get me into all kinds of trouble that would be worth it. Instead, I held his gaze as I stared him down. When he didn't respond, I couldn't resist throwing fuel onto the fire by teasing him. "What's the matter? Cat got your tongue?" I flashed my fangs at him as I grinned.

Rei gripped the armrests of his throne so hard that the gilded wood creaked. He shifted his gaze away from me to the young royal, who had played his part as an ardent fan to perfection so far. "I'm sure Prince Renner is exhausted after such a tiring journey." Rei gestured, summoning two servants. "They will escort you to your room, where you can rest until we meet for dinner later."

The young royal bowed. "That is very kind of you, Your Majesty. I look forward to spending the evening getting better acquainted." He flicked his gaze over to me. "I hope our paths cross again soon, Cheshire."

"You can be sure of it, young princeling."

Prince Renner bowed before he left with his guards, diplomat, and accompanying servants to go to his guest quarters.

Rei's rage was practically sparking. His voice was a dark rumble as he demanded, "What in the seven hearts of Hell do you think you're doing?"

I shrugged nonchalantly. "Why are you so upset? I was a well-behaved gentleman and perfectly civil to the little prince. Isn't that what you wanted?"

He narrowed his eyes at me. "What I want is for you to stay away from him."

I approached him with a sway of my hips as my tail flicked behind me. "That sure sounds like jealousy to me."

"Don't be absurd." Rei scoffed, as if it was the most ridiculous accusation in the world.

"You're just mad because he liked me more than you." I sprawled out in Rei's lap, draping my arms over his neck to support myself. "If you send that charming boy home, you can have me all to yourself."

My heart rejoiced when he automatically wrapped his arms around me to hold me closer. "You know I can't do that."

"No, you *won't* do that, which is different." I pouted as I looked up at him. "Why are you going through with this farce? When the prince is so sweet, it will make you feel bad to go through this stupid interview just to turn him down because you're too in love with me. Your denial is making it worse."

"I've never denied the fact that my heart belongs to you, Chess," Rei said softly, stroking my arm with his thumb. "If I didn't love you more than life itself, I wouldn't struggle so much."

It was equal parts sweet and frustrating. "Then when are you going to choose me and happiness instead of being alone and miserable?"

He looked at me with those wounded puppy eyes that broke my heart. "Please don't make this harder than it needs to be."

It was impossible to hold in my frustrated sigh. "I miss the days when you were actually happy to see me and not so vexed every time I appear." I gestured around us. "There's no one even here, yet you won't even indulge me with one kiss."

Rei's gaze dropped to my lips. "Because one kiss will lead to one hundred more."

"And the problem with that is what?" When Rei started with the same tired protests, I cut him off. "If the prince is a fan of mine, then doesn't that prove the tide has turned on people's opinion of me?"

"He is a sheltered boy who knows nothing of the real world." The bitterness in Rei's voice tugged on my heartstrings. "It's only natural that stories of your misadventures would excite a child trapped in a palace with no hopes of ascending to the throne."

It felt too cruel to point out that Rei had been that same carefree soul when I first met him as the young third prince who was never meant to be king. I tried to distract him instead. "If only he knew the truth about our sexy 'misadventures' we used to have." I nuzzled against Rei's neck, earning me a sharp inhale. "Come on, let's go upstairs to start some new rumors."

Before he could answer, the doors to the throne room opened, revealing Bianco with Alistair at his side. The human was remarkably unassuming, considering he was the savior of Wonderland who had restored magic and shifters by forming a mating bond with the White Rabbit. Unlike my stubborn love, Alistair always was happy to see me.

"We're sorry to interrupt," Bianco said with a smirk that suggested otherwise. "But you'll be late for your meeting with Hatter, Vivalter, and March if you don't leave soon."

I hugged Rei tighter. "My dear brother and his friends can wait. I'm not letting my darling leave until I get at least one kiss."

Rei leaned down to press a gentle kiss to my forehead that melted me like an icy treat left outside on a hot summer day. But I wasn't about to let him get away with that. Before he could move away, I pulled him down for a passionate kiss on the lips.

When he drew back, I grinned at him. "You owe me at least ninety-nine more."

"I have no doubt you'll come to collect in full." He fondly ruffled my hair, making me want him to pet me all over. It was a much nicer alternative than him being cross with me for taking such liberties. But how could he be mad at me for giving him what he really wanted?

"You'd expect nothing less from me." I shifted into my cat form and jumped off his lap to go over to rub against Bianco's and then Alistair's legs. "At least two people are always happy to have me around. Hello again, dear friends."

Because he was the best, the human picked me up for a proper cuddle that had me purring loudly as I nuzzled against his cheek with all the affection I held in my heart for him. It was nice that he never rejected my platonic love for him. Having Rei scowl with jealousy was also a fun bonus.

It was easy to be self-indulgent with Alistair when he was so generous with his petting. "I haven't seen you around for a while. What have you been up to?"

"Oh, a little of this, a lot of that. You know how it goes." I headbutted his hand to demand more

scritches behind my ears, which he gladly gave me.
"I'm being a very good boy, but I'm not getting any
credit for it. It's all quite tragic."

"Does that mean you've left the prince alone?"
Alistair's surprise showed how well he had come to
know me since he had arrived in Wonderland.

"It's hard to hate him when he's so very charming." I harrumphed in annoyance, even though I had
chosen to let him be my unexpected ally. "The churl
should have the decency to be the troll I was expecting, but alas."

"Is that your game?" Rei regarded me with suspicion. "You're pretending to like him to catch me off
guard when you inevitably start plotting a way to
chase him off?"

I pretended to act aghast. "I'm appalled you say
that, as if I would do something so underhanded."

Bianco cleared his throat. "Your Majesty, they're
waiting."

Rei heaved a resigned sigh as he stood. "Fine.
Cheshire, I want none of your shenanigans with
Prince Renner. Keep your distance, understood?"

I flattened my ears in irritation that he used my
full name. "What's my reward for good behavior?"

"Do what I ask, and you'll find out." Rei walked
down the steps of the dais. It was impossible not to

admire his fine form, which looked stunning in his metallic red tunic trimmed with gold that was paired with tight black britches that showed off why his shapely ass was a national treasure.

Although I hated the sight of him walking away from me with Bianco, I at least enjoyed the view as I peered over Alistair's shoulder until they were gone.

My friend gave me the hug I desperately needed. I shifted into my human form to take full advantage of the comfort. While he was smaller than me, he embraced me with his entire soul.

He looked up at me with concern when I pulled back. "Are you doing okay? It can't be easy having Prince Renner here."

"Something tells me it'll all work out for the best." I was determined to will that optimism into being the truth. "I've already gotten away with more in the last two days than I have in the last three years, so there's hope for me yet."

"Really? That's great!" He radiated genuine joy for me, which was a balm to my battered soul. "I was planning on introducing myself to the prince later to do some recon for you."

I hugged Alistair again. "You truly are a wonderful friend." I stepped back as I gave him my famous playful grin. "But I'm off to go check on the prince myself right now."

He laughed. "I'd expect nothing less. Call me if you need reinforcements. You know I've always got your back."

"I do, and I'm forever grateful." I gave his shoulder a fond squeeze before I used my magic to turn invisible. It was so much easier to get up to fun mischief when nobody could see you.

"Whatever you're going to say, just say it." I could feel Bianco's gaze on me as we walked through the halls of my palace.

His expression was one of pure innocence, but we had known each other for too many years for me to believe that. "That kiss did not seem like the first in three years."

I scowled at how observant my friend was. "And?"

"And I'm happy for you both."

It was sweet, but it also was a reminder of how much I had slipped with Cheshire. "My mistake was slipping once. Now, it is harder than ever to control myself around him."

"That's not a bad thing."

The issue was more than I was comfortable discussing when the walls had a tendency to have ears. "I must be more careful." Putting the thought of the troublesome cat shifter out of my mind, I shifted my mindset to be ready for my meeting. "Is Vivalter attending by invitation or his own initiative?" To my knowledge, we had made the appointment only for Hatter and March to talk about a new commission.

"I'm sure he has his reasons for accompanying them."

I frowned at the answer. "Those reasons are usually cryptic, frustrating, and ominous." The butterfly shifter rarely put my mind at ease with his predictions about the future.

"Perhaps he has some insights into the Prince Renner situation."

I wasn't sure if that would be a comfort or source of worry. But I tried to settle my nerves as I entered my private chambers. Hatter, Vivalter, and March were waiting at the long table, which had been set with a modest afternoon tea party. They all stood as I entered, but I gestured for them to sit. Despite being a ruler, I couldn't stand all the pomp and circumstance that went along with the role.

"Welcome. I hope you're all well," I greeted them

before taking a seat at the head of the table. Bianco sat to my right as my most trusted advisor and friend.

"It is always a wonderful day when we get to pay you a visit," Hatter said. It amazed me he could say such grand things without sounding smarmy. The man was elegance personified, in his impeccably tailored three-piece teal suit paired with a vibrant purple shirt and lavender tie. His turquoise hair was pulled back in a partial bun, with the rest falling around his handsome face.

March gave me a friendly smile. "It's a pleasure to be back here." He usually was away handling Hatter's business affairs, so it had been some time since his last visit. Quiet and unassuming, it was easy for March to blend into the background. But like Bianco, he was a keen observer who saw everything, making him a powerful asset for Hatter.

Vivalter looked ethereal and mysterious in his glimmering gossamer robes and his blond-and-pastel rainbow hair framing his face. Sometimes I couldn't believe he was Cheshire's older brother, and at other times, their similarities were all too clear. "Please forgive my presumptuousness in inviting myself to the gathering."

I waved away his concerns. "You always have a standing invitation to visit me at the palace. It is your right as the royal seer to come and go as you please." I took a deep breath before asking the question I most feared. "Is there something in particular that brought you here today?"

"It has begun."

I gritted my teeth to prevent my expression from reflecting my irritation with his cryptic comments. "What has?"

"The changes."

That illuminated about as much as the night with no moon. "Could you be more specific?"

"Oh, I'm quite certain you're *very* aware of what I'm speaking of without further elaboration." His knowing smirk drove his point home.

It brought heat to my cheeks as I cleared my throat. While I was curious if he had found out from Cheshire himself or visions, I refrained from fully exposing my situation to all present. "What of them?"

"He is doing what he must, and you must do what you should. It is the only way to find happiness for you and your kingdom."

A pit of dread formed in my stomach. The thing I *should* do was accept Prince Renner as my consort, but I would never do that when Cheshire held my heart. "And if I cannot do as I should?"

"A cowardly king does not have an easy future on

the throne." There was a hint of disapproval in his tone that sent a shudder through me. "A choice *must* be made to ensure the future."

My heart sank. It must have shown on my face because his expression and tone softened. "Sometimes what we should do aligns with what we want."

"Is now one of those times?" Because I really needed it to be one of those times.

"It can be if you continue on your current path."

As always, his cryptic words made me want to bash my head into the nearest stone wall until I lost consciousness. Because his words gave me hope that giving in to Cheshire was something I needed to do more of, but everything he had said up to that point implied otherwise. "I fear the world has not changed as much as required for me to find true happiness."

"The world has changed more than you would think," March said with a quiet confidence. "Now that shifters have returned along with the magic, it has forced a reckoning. It has been heartening to see far more acceptance in my travels than prejudiced rejection."

"But there is a difference between shifters and Cheshire." I frowned with frustration over the reality of the situation. "There is far more distrust surrounding him than shifters in general."

"Only from those who have not had the good fortune to meet him," Hatter said. "Cheshire could charm even the most curmudgeonly doubter."

"As our king has firsthand experience with," Vivalter added with a hint of a grin that reminded me of his brother's infamous one.

Bianco did a poor job of covering his laugh behind his hand.

I scowled but shifted topics instead. "And what of Prince Renner? What's his role in all of this?"

"He will not only be a powerful ally, but he'll be the harbinger of true love for you," Vivalter predicted.

His prediction sent icy dread through me. "In what manner?"

"I told you before that Prince Renner will bring you many gifts, including the greatest love of all."

The thought was unfathomable when my heart belonged only to Cheshire. "I will never love that whelp of a boy."

"He will win you over." When I protested, Vivalter held up his hand to silence me. "Might I remind you that there are many ways to love? It applies to these matters."

"I'm incapable of loving him romantically." That was something I vehemently believed about Prince Renner. "Nor even as one adores a younger brother."

"He's only just arrived. Give it time."

I didn't want to do that, though. His charmed reactions to Cheshire left me unsettled. What if his interest in the cat shifter ran deeper than a mere infatuation with the tales of his mischief? Could Prince Renner be in love with Cheshire? Surely not.

"Come, let us not dwell on such unpleasant things," Hatter said. "I would much rather hear about what Your Majesty would like me to design for your next gala ball."

It was a safer topic, despite the thought of attending a formal function made me want to groan with grief. I hated such overwrought celebrations when I was rarely in the mood to be joyous. Until I was free to be with Cheshire, there was nothing for me to celebrate.

But would I ever be allowed to follow my heart to him?

"Do you think we did enough to inspire King Rei to act?" Prince Renner asked once I arrived in his room. He toyed with his lower lip as we sat on his bed. "I fear we may have been too subtle."

Shifting into my human form, I tossed my hair over my shoulder. "After you left, I stole a kiss he didn't reject, so it at least worked a little."

The young royal lit up with genuine delight. "Really? That's great!"

"It would have been even better if his duties hadn't interrupted us." My tail swished behind me with annoyance. "But we seem to have left him unsettled, which is a good start. The next step will be selling your infatuation with me."

He nodded in agreement. "Dinner will be the perfect opportunity for that. I can express interest by asking him all kinds of questions about you, which is sure to stir his jealous nature."

"I'm *so* going to enjoy watching from the sidelines." The thought of Rei clamping down on his annoyance delighted me.

Prince Renner heaved an envious sigh. "You're so lucky you can turn invisible! I can only imagine how useful that is for sneaking out of places you don't want to be."

"And into places I'm not welcomed," I added. "You don't strike me as the type who wants to hide, though."

"I'm invisible to my parents until they have a political use for me." Prince Renner straightened a wrinkle in the heart-print duvet cover. "I'd like to think my life was worth more than being a convenient marriage arrangement, but that seems to be the only value I have to them."

It was impossible not to feel for the young man. "I'm sorry they can't see that you're worth so much more than that."

"I wish I was brave enough to run away and leave it all behind. It sounds romantic and fun, but I'm also realistic enough to understand I'm very sheltered and not at all equipped to be out in the real world because of my upbringing." He sighed as he leaned back on his hands. "I want to live a life of adventure I read about in books, but I'd feel a lot safer doing it with someone who loved me by my side to guide me."

"Wow, so you're still a hopeless romantic despite your lot in life?" I teased him. "I'm impressed."

His cheeks flushed pink. "I know it's naïve of me, but I..."

My gaze softened as I looked at him. "There's nothing wrong with wanting to be loved. It's good to have dreams about being whisked away to a life of adventure. It gives you hope."

"Exactly. I just want to do something myself that matters and has nothing to do with who I was born to be. It makes me sound like an idealistic ninny, but I want someone to love me for who I am and not because of my title or status."

"You should settle for nothing less because that's what you deserve." I brushed my tail against the back of his hand in friendly comfort. "Someone as kind as you deserves genuine love and not a marriage of convenience to someone who wants to use you for your political connections. This Cheshire cat swears he'll help you avoid that fate."

Prince Renner looked at me with such hopeful eyes. "Really?"

"Consider it your reward. It's the least I can do for you helping me win Rei over."

His sweet smile was sure to win the heart of whoever was lucky enough to end up with him. "You're as amazing as all the legends say. I'm glad you're real and even better than all the tales promised."

"You and I shall have fun, young princeling. But Rei is right, you should rest before dinner. I'll leave you to it."

"Where are you going?"

My natural curiosity had gotten the better of me, so I would need to take a slight detour. "I have something to take care of first before I join you from the shadows to watch dinner. We shall talk again soon, though."

With those words, I disappeared and went in search of my older sibling. I could sense him through our familial bond, which I used to entice him to come meet with me alone.

I waited in a private bedroom in the royal wing for Vivalter to appear with a scowl. "Did you need to summon me now?"

"Is that any way to greet your favorite brother?" I

wagged my tail with enjoyment at teasing my sibling. "You know you want to indulge my curiosity."

"You certainly wasted no time in playing games with the young prince."

I shrugged. "What's wrong with that? You foretold our paths crossing. I just sped things up a little."

"Truthfully, I am surprised you chose to team up with Prince Renner instead of working to chase him away."

My brother's mysterious powers were beyond my understanding, so I didn't question how he already knew about my plans. "Have you ruined the surprise for our dear king?"

Vivalter shook his head. "He needs to have his realizations on his own time. It would only hurt him if I were to interfere in the process."

"Are you willing to indulge my curiosity about the little princeling?"

His indigo eyes studied me carefully. "Regarding what specifically?"

"Does he get to live his life of adventure with the person who loves him for him?" It seemed tremendously important.

My brother tucked his blond-and-rainbow hair behind his ear. "What difference would it make to you?"

"Despite my intentions to hate the brat, I can't help but be fond of him when he is so kind and true." I sighed in defeat. "It's most vexing."

"The game has begun, but the players have not yet met. A few more things must happen first before they can be brought together."

Parsing between the lines of my brother's cryptic hints was as frustrating as ever. "Who will be his romantic partner?"

"A fated mate."

I arched my eyebrows in shock at the information. Prince Renner was destined to end up with a shifter? "Is it someone I know?"

"All I can say is it will come as a surprise to all involved."

That meant my brother would refuse to elaborate further on the identity, so it was time to switch tracks with my line of questioning. "But if it's a fated mate, that means it will eventually lead to true love, right?"

"If everything happens as it should." Vivalter nodded to himself with a pleased hum. "And it will certainly spawn an interesting adventure if it plays out the way I've foreseen."

"What about me?"

He gave me a disapproving look. "You know there

is no point in discussing your future when you are an agent of chaos who is impenetrable to my gaze."

"Are we really playing this old game?" I rolled my eyes at his predictable answer. "You know when I ask about myself, I'm asking about Rei."

The corners of Vivalter's mouth turned upward in a slight smirk. "I don't need the ability to see the future to see the two of you have certainly gotten under his skin today."

"But will that get me to where I want to be with him?" It was pointless to ask my brother such a question when he'd refuse to give me a straight answer, but I still had to try.

"I won't dissuade you from your current plan. But take care you do not push him too hard. He is a man who is already at his breaking point. You do not wish to shatter him."

"Just his resistance to us being together." I sighed at how impossible my task seemed. "Can't you give your dear baby brother an ounce of comfort in these uncertain times?"

Vivalter's gaze softened as he gestured for me to come closer. It was a rare invitation, so I gladly accepted his embrace, nuzzling against him with a purr of contentment.

He gave me a scratch behind my cat ears. "You are

the only person capable of writing their own fate and turning all of my predictions upside down. If you wish for King Rei to be yours, you must make it so."

"But how much longer do I have to fight?" I sagged into the comfort of my brother's hug. "I'm so very tired, Vivalter. I just want to be happily in love with Rei again."

"You are far closer to your goal than you were. The only thing I know for certain is he cannot be yours until you tell him he is indeed your fated mate. Without that knowledge, he cannot make his choice."

I burrowed against my brother's neck, taking comfort in the scent of the heady herbs he smoked to help him see his visions that guided the kingdom. They made me light-headed and tingly in the best of ways. "While I know you're right, it doesn't make it any less scary." I had a deep fear that Rei would leave me for good if he found out that fate had deemed him mine. He resented fate for putting him on the throne and wouldn't take kindly to it dictating who he was supposed to love.

"And in all these years, it never occurred to you that finding out he's your fated mate might make it easier for him to choose you?"

"I wish it was that easy." Life would be so much simpler if it were true.

Vivalter gave me a tight squeeze before he pulled away from me. "Do not falter in your desires when you're so close to finally getting what you want."

I strengthened my resolve. "Of course, you're right. You're always right. It is a most infuriating trait."

"And one you share. Imagine that." He grinned at me, making me laugh.

"Speaking of which, when will you quit running away from your fated mate?" It was a sore subject for Vivalter but worth bringing up. "Hatter must be so tired of waiting."

"Like you, good timing is key. But my problems are my own. Do not deflect your issues by focusing on mine."

I grinned at him. "Hey, it was worth a try."

"While I know dangerous things happen when you're left to entertain yourself, I must return to the king."

I accepted that as an invitation to accompany him, as I trailed behind in my invisible form as he returned to Rei's personal chambers.

"Is everything okay, Vivi?" Hatter asked with concern, looking up from his sketchbook, which was spread over the long table.

Vivalter took a seat with a small sigh. "Yes, apart

from my brother insisting now was the most opportune time for me to satisfy his burning curiosities about Prince Renner."

From my hidden vantage point, I didn't miss the way Rei's eyes narrowed at the mention of the name. "And what did Cheshire wish to know about him?"

"Whether Prince Renner would find his happily ever after." Vivalter gave an unconcerned shrug. It surprised me when my brother knew I was silently observing the scene.

Clearly used to dealing with my older sibling's vagaries, Rei clarified. "Did Cheshire ask about who Prince Renner's partner would be?"

"Yes, he had some concerns about their identity."

An interesting mix of emotions flickered across Rei's face before he settled back into a neutral mask. "Why?"

"Because he does not believe that you are meant to be with Prince Renner and wished for some reassurance."

"Does Cheshire think he's supposed to be the prince's partner?" The agony in Rei's voice broke my heart. He looked stricken by the mere possibility.

I wanted to go over to him and tell him he didn't need to worry about me being with anyone. However, for our plan to work, he needed to sit with those fears and use them to help him decide to choose me.

"Is that a concern for you?" Vivalter asked, never taking his gaze off the king.

"Prince Renner seemed smitten today when they met, and Cheshire was certainly enjoying the attention." Rei scowled at the memory. "It was uncomfortable. And…"

"And?" Vivalter prompted when the king trailed off.

"And Cheshire's never mentioned me being his fated mate. Now that Prince Renner is here, I wonder if…"

Bianco interjected when Rei once again drifted into silence. "Have you ever talked to Cheshire about his fated mate?"

"No, but after you and Alistair bonded, it made me curious about who Cheshire's fated mate would be since all shifters apparently have them. Surely, as long as we've been together, he would have told me if it was me, right?"

Bianco's gaze shifted over to me before returning to the king. "That is a conversation you should have with him. I believe you would find it most enlightening." He looked over at me again to drive home his point, causing me to flatten my ears. I knew the

White Rabbit shifter could scent me, even in my invisible form. I hated that he was right about Rei and I needing to talk about the uncomfortable subject.

Rei frowned. "But he's known me all one hundred and fifty-six years of my existence. If I was his fated mate, why wouldn't he tell me?"

"Because it is not as simple as that. And when you are a man who resents fate for your lot in life, it would not be an easy thing to tell you that same force is responsible for him being your mate," Bianco said before hastily adding, "if that's the case."

"It is a conversation you should have had years ago, but it is not too late." Vivalter sent a pointed look in my direction as well. "But I would urge you to remember that while fate sets our paths, we have the free will to deviate. Rejected mates are rare but do exist. So, it is not as clear-cut as fate says you will be mates, and that is the end of the story."

"It's a wonderful thing, though." Bianco's smile spoke of how satisfied he was with his bonded mate, Alistair. I was happy for them yet envious of the ease with which they lived in harmony. "As your friend, I would remind you to keep an open mind when you talk to Cheshire later."

"Everything Cheshire has done has been out of love for you," March said in a quiet voice. I appreciated his show of support. "Perhaps you will question everything else, but you never need to doubt the depths of his genuine adoration for you."

Rei rubbed his temples with a sigh. "This ordeal is giving me a headache. How soon until I can send Prince Renner away and get back to my normal life?"

"You will never return to the way things were before," Vivalter predicted. "They've already changed forever."

"In that case, I suggest we take a break from all the taxing thoughts and heavy talk. What do you think of this sketch, Your Majesty?" Hatter held up his drawing of an outfit for the king's approval.

I lingered a little longer, but now that I wasn't the subject of discussion, my attention wandered. It was clear I needed to retreat and start planning for an awkward conversation later. Why had I waited so long to talk to him about being my fated mate? Would my stupidity cost me the mate I loved so dearly?

Prince Renner's boyish youthfulness made me feel far older than my one hundred and fifty-six years. Everything had become so heavy since my coronation that it weighed me down until I could hardly move at all. But I struggled through it to atone for the atrocities my mother and oldest brother had inflicted on the good people of the Kingdom of Hearts. I owed it to my citizens to be a magnanimous ruler who reigned with dignity and fairness, until all memory of my predecessors' misdeeds had been forgotten. While it was the right thing to do, it didn't make it any easier to choose duty over the person my heart wanted most but couldn't have.

Pushing my somber thoughts aside, I focused on

Prince Renner as he entered my dining room. He looked like a fresh-faced young man who had never seen a day of hardship in his life. I couldn't help but be a little envious of his lightness. "Thank you for joining me, Prince Renner."

He sat down across from me with a bubbly smile. "Oh, it is my pleasure! I must thank you for such wonderful accommodations. The comforts of my room here put mine to shame. If it weren't so uncouth, I'd beg to take the mattress back with me."

I chuckled at his reaction as the servants served dinner. "I'm glad you're so comfortable here already."

"It's going to be a challenge not to get spoiled during my stay." He held up his wineglass in a toast. "You have my sincerest appreciation for being such a wonderful host."

I lifted my glass in return. "May you enjoy your time here in my kingdom." We were too far apart to clink our drinks together, so we sipped them instead.

"Perhaps it is poor form to admit it, but I dare say I'm already enjoying myself too much." Prince Renner waited for me to take a bite of the Jubjub bird dumplings before sampling his own. He made a soft sound of pleasure. "This is so sumptuously delicious! You are spoiling me, Your Majesty."

"It is my honor to take care of people." It was

something I prided myself on after the selfish reign of my mother, the former Queen of Hearts.

"You do it well. I can see why you are so beloved by your people. To have a king who cares about others is a very good ruler, indeed."

I tilted my head in acknowledgment of the praise. "It is my sincerest hope that my legacy be one of kindness and caring. I never want anyone to fear me like they did my mother and oldest brother. While I can't undo what they did in the past, I'm determined to atone for it by treating the citizens of my kingdom well."

The prince gazed at me with genuine admiration. "In three short years, you've already done so much to help others. I admire that about you." His expression turned thoughtful. "My father isn't unkind, but he is *very* strict. He's obsessed with everything being done in a certain way to keep control over everyone. My personal theory is that some part of him fears the people will rise against him if they think he's too soft, like they did to the Looking-Glass Land royal family."

"Although I was a child when the revolution happened, the former rulers' ostentatious over-spending on lavish parties at the expense of people starving had far more to do with why they were dethroned. It is most likely why your parents are known for being so austere with their expenditures."

The corner of his mouth turned up in a wry grin. "Don't I know it? As the sixth son, everything of mine is hand-me-downs. There is precious little I've ever had that's new and just for me. It's why I'm so envious of the fashionable clothing I've seen since I arrived. Both your suit and Cheshire's are beyond exquisite."

"Hatter Merveilles is the designer we both choose to wear. I would be happy to arrange a meeting for you so he could design something for you while you're here."

His expression turned wistful. "I'd love to accept such a generous offer, but my father would disown me when I got back home if I bought something so extravagant. Not even the first son gets to wear such luxurious outfits."

That simply wouldn't do. "Consider it an early gift for your Coming of Age ceremony."

He waved his hands in front of him. "But that's too much, Your Majesty!"

I gestured for a servant to come over. "Please send a letter to Hatter requesting his services for Prince Renner here at the palace tomorrow." He bowed his head and scurried away to take care of it at once.

Prince Renner looked at me in awe. "Thank you doesn't seem like an adequate expression for such a generous gift. I am honored and touched, Your Majesty." He took a sip of his wine as our dishes were cleared and the next course was served. "It seems at least some of the rumors about you are true."

"There tends to be a kernel of truth in most of them." I savored a bite of my boar beast roast with polongoberry sauce.

"They say that twice a month, you open your court to your people to listen to their problems and offer help. If someone's child is sick, you give them the money they need for treatment and even access to the best doctors in your kingdom."

I nodded. "That one is actually true. Nobody should suffer because of a lack of funds or they live too far away from a good doctor. Taking care of them is a far better use of that money than it simply gathering dust in the treasury, waiting for some future war I have no intention of fighting. My money is there to help take care of my people. Plus, as it is from the taxes they paid, it rightfully should go back to them."

"My father could learn a *lot* from you if he wasn't so damn stubborn and set in his ways." Prince Renner hummed with contentment as he continued enjoying his meal. "You really are amazing. And so is this food."

"Most of that money was collected by my mother with unfair taxes that harmed the people. I'm uncomfortable with profiting from anyone's suffering, so it's my way of giving it back to those who need it most." It was one of the many ways I tried to counteract the harm my family had caused everyone. "My mother was especially unkind to Hatter, so it was important to me to help him rebuild his business to undo what damage I could. I am fortunate that he's a forgiving soul who doesn't hold my family's sins against me. He has become an excellent friend to me."

"I can't wait to meet him. Word of his legendary tea parties has reached even our kingdom."

Something wasn't adding up to me. "You seem to hear an awful lot of gossip and rumors for a prince. Normally, they are unconcerned with such things unless they're the topic of conversation."

The young royal blushed so hard it reached the tips of his ears. "As the sixth son and twelfth child, I'm invisible to my family until they have a use for me, like marrying me off. Since my siblings were all older than me, I was alone most of the time. My only friends were the servants in the palace who took care of me."

"It says a lot about your character that you befriended them." My esteem for him went up quite a few notches.

"They're just as invisible as me, so we had more in common than you'd expect." He took a sip of wine. "They knew I loved reading and wanted to travel beyond the palace walls, but my father forbade us from going anywhere because it was too expensive. Because of that, the servants always filled me in on the latest gossip and rumors they heard, to give me a window to the world I wanted to be a part of."

"So *that's* why you're so well informed about what goes on in my kingdom?"

"Tarabithea's family lives here, so whenever she visits them here, she brings back the best stories about the Kingdom of Hearts." He hung his head with a sheepish expression. "I know idle gossip is a terrible thing to be interested in, especially when rumors can be harmful sometimes. But it's the only way I hear about what happens in the real world outside my locked cage. It sounds pathetic, but coming here is the first time I've ever left Mirrorland."

The pieces began slotting together. "Thus, why you are so fascinated by the stories about Cheshire."

His expression brightened with excitement.

"They're my favorite! I had never met a shifter before today, so his ability to shapeshift between human and cat form was the stuff of my wildest dreams. To be powerful enough to still use magic when it had disappeared from Wonderland amazed me. I would dream about meeting him and seeing him use his powers, especially against those awful aristocrats who treated me with the same disdain they reserved for the servants."

"He takes particular relish in taunting the members of my court who don't approve of him, no matter how many times I tell him to leave them alone." I shook my head with a rueful sigh. "But as I'm sure you know, cats are not very good at doing what they're told. Especially one as stubborn and strong-willed as him. But it's hard to get mad at him when they annoy me, too."

Prince Renner hid a laugh behind his hand. "They do?"

"Like you, I was the third son, who was invisible because all the focus went to the heir and spare. I was seen as weak and idealistic, so my family had no use for me. The aristocrats had nothing but snide words for me back then. But when I was forced to take the throne, those same people were all too quick to kiss my ring. Their fake support and overt fawning that my mother had trained them to shower her with is a practice I'll never be comfortable engaging in. I have no patience for false flattery or pomp and circumstance."

"It's the *worst*," Prince Renner groaned in commiseration. "I'd rather hang out with the servants than those stuffy aristocrats any day of the week. At least they like me for me. I never have to doubt that because my father certainly doesn't pay them enough to pretend to care about anyone but him, my mother, and the heir."

I didn't intend to say anything, but the words escaped me without permission. "Cheshire was my only real friend when I was younger. He was the only person who didn't mock me for wanting to make things better for people."

The prince turned hesitant. "Am I allowed to ask how you two met, or is that too forward and none of my business?"

"It's fine. I hated being in the castle and listening to my mother and brother's violence. Regan was always holed up in his bedroom with his studies, so I would go out and explore by myself to get away from it all." It had been my sole refuge back then. "I was wandering around the forest when our paths crossed. I wanted nothing to do with his antics, so of course, that made him want me to pay attention to him twice as much."

"In true cat fashion."

I snorted in amusement. "Absolutely. But he was quick to show me he didn't have the normal feline aversion to water." Skinny-dipping in Lake Wibbly Bibbly with Cheshire was one of my fondest memories from back then. Few things were as romantic as kissing under the waterfall, without a single care in the world, as long as we were together. My heart ached for those long-gone days. "No one had ever been playful or teased me before, so it took some getting used to. But he gradually pulled me out of my shell. The only time I was truly happy was when I was with him back then."

"Then is it true that you two were lovers?" My hesitation to answer told him everything. His expression shifted into a sympathetic one that made my suppressed emotions tremble. "But you had to give him up for the crown."

"Because of his reputation as a trickster shifter, my people fear him. They certainly would never accept him as my consort. And I swore an oath to my citizens that I would never put my needs above theirs. To choose him over my royal duties would be the height of selfishness and break the trust I've worked so hard to build."

"I know I'm way out of line here, but has it occurred to you that everyone would be more willing to accept it now *because* you've built that trust? After everything you've done to make their lives better, your people want to see you be happy, too. I can't imagine anyone begrudging the kindest King of Hearts being in love, even if it is with a shifter."

His naivety was sweet. "If it were that simple, I would have done it by now."

"Respectfully, as someone who has heard an absurd amount of gossip from the common people, Alistair's miracle of returning the magic to Wonderland through his mating bond has changed many people's opinions on shifters. Master Bianco is well respected and held in high esteem for what he helped his mate do and his undying loyalty to you. Shifters have returned, and people aren't scared now that they realize they're just like everyone else."

"Cheshire is different. His centuries of mischief have created a deep mistrust with everyone. It's why my family forbid me from marrying him."

Prince Renner bit his lip as he seemed to debate what to say next. "Please tell me if I'm overstepping, but from what I know, your mom mistrusted *everyone*. She probably feared his magic being powerful enough to overthrow her, if that was Cheshire's desire. And she would have had a vested interest in keeping you unmarried so she could use you to build an alliance."

I had to concede his point. "Fair. My happiness was never her priority."

"Has anyone on your *current* staff that you *trust* told you that marrying Cheshire is forbidden? Or have any of your people on those open court days where they come talk to you raised concerns about the Cheshire cat terrorizing anyone?"

I blinked several times as I processed his questions. "Not exactly."

"Take it from someone who has made it his goal to hear every fantastical tale about Cheshire. All the stories are about how he uses his magical powers to toy with the awful aristocrats who cause problems. He *never* harms regular people and helps them when their paths cross. I can tell you that commoners think he's an amazing folk hero. I promise you, Cheshire is revered, not feared."

Part of me wanted to trust what he was saying, but it was too good to be true. "I find that difficult to believe when Diplomat Marram made it *very* clear she had heard all the 'disgusting' rumors about me and Cheshire."

Prince Renner rolled his eyes in a theatrical way that reminded me of how young he was. "Marram thinks *everything* is disgusting. She wants to live in a world where everyone is as awful and miserable as her. She's the *worst*."

"I can't say I disagree. It was good fortune that she wasn't here for this trip."

"It was *such* a relief." Prince Renner laughed as I joined him with a chuckle. "Sure, someone like her who rubs elbows with all the aristocrats is going to have negative feelings about him. But people like her don't matter, as much as she likes to think she's the most important person in the kingdom after my parents."

"I'm impressed," I said. "You make a very convincing argument, but I still find it difficult to accept that Cheshire is anything but feared."

He perked up with a sudden burst of excitement. "I have an idea! You're probably going to tell me no, but it's the best way to prove my point."

I gestured for him to speak. "You've sufficiently intrigued me. What's your plan?"

He leaned forward with a glimmer in his seafoam-green eyes. "If you're up for a little adventure, why don't we dress up in disguises and go to the local tavern? I'm sure we can casually bring up Cheshire, and you can hear from the townsfolk themselves what they think. It'll prove that they like him more than they fear him. And then you can be with him!"

I studied him carefully, trying to figure out what he was hoping to accomplish. "Wouldn't that defeat the point of our marriage interview?"

"Forgive me for saying this, but things would be very different if your heart didn't belong to Cheshire. But when you love him, there's no place here for me, even though you are the perfect man I've always dreamed of loving in every other way."

Despite being unwilling to change the situation, I still felt guilty for not being the man he needed. When he was so kind and caring, it felt like a failing on my part. "My apologies. It wasn't fair to bring you here when I knew from the beginning it would never work."

"Not fair?" He scoffed. "Please, this is the *best* thing that's ever happened to me! Because my father trusts you, I was allowed to *leave the palace.* I got to travel for the first time and meet Cheshire! I'm literally living the dream right now. Having a covert adventure like the ones I've always read about and seeing how the townspeople live is an amazing consolation prize."

I chuckled at his boyish enthusiasm. "It's a pity. Under different circumstances, we would have been well suited for each other."

"I'm happy to settle for being a friend." His genuine smile was impossible not to return. "So, what do you say? Can we go have a fun night out on the town in disguise?"

"It's a wildly brazen and foolish plan." However, I was still tempted despite my instincts that told me it was a bad idea. Because what if Prince Renner was right? What if the only thing that had been standing in my way had been my inherited biases I never thought to question?

His expression fell until I continued. "But I suppose there really is no better way to find out than straight from the source."

He grew hopeful again. "Does that mean we can do it?"

"Zatinger, would you please come here?" I requested. My bodyguard emerged from the shadows, making Prince Renner yelp in surprise. The man's ability to blend into the scenery made Zatinger excellent at his job. He had been with me since the beginning and knew all my secrets.

He bowed low. "Yes, Your Majesty?"

"Would you be willing to act as our guide and take us to your local tavern for a little reconnaissance?"

He gave me a wolfish grin. "It would be my honor. But you'll definitely need to change. I'll have appropriate clothes sent to both of your rooms."

"We would appreciate it."

He bowed again before leaving to tend to his task.

I wiped the corner of my mouth with a napkin before setting it on the table. "Well, it looks like you'll get your wish to have an adventure."

He pumped the air with his fist. "This will be *so* much fun! You won't regret this."

"In that case, I suppose we should go prepare to change." Despite my apprehensions, I couldn't help but grow excited. It had been a *very* long time since I had tried to blend in with the townsfolk.

Could I be lucky enough to discover that Prince Renner was right? There was only one way to find out.

" **I** must admit, I'm very impressed, little princeling," I said after Prince Renner was alone in his room and finished changing. I revealed myself in cat form as I made myself comfortable on his bed. "You went off script, but what a delightful result you earned for your efforts. I never would have expected Rei to agree to such outlandish shenanigans."

"That he agreed to go shows how much he wants me to be right." He looked in the mirror as he straightened the navy tunic over his tan britches. "I'm amazed he didn't shut me down and tell me to stop sticking my nose where it didn't belong. I can't believe I was so bold!"

"You have my gratitude for trying to make him

see his fears are based on old ghosts that deserve to be banished to the past."

He sat on the edge of the bed beside me. "Are you coming with us?"

I grinned at him. "Of course! I'd die of curiosity if I didn't, which simply isn't my style. But I promise to stay invisible because I don't want Rei to think I've influenced anyone he speaks with. For once, I will be a good boy and remain a passive observer." I headbutted his hand in a bid for attention.

"Am I allowed to pet you?" Prince Renner asked uncertainly.

"Yes, you've earned it." I nuzzled against him again, which earned me the scritches behind my ear that I so loved. "Thank you for being a good friend, Prince Renner. It's been a very long time since I've had a new one."

He stroked my head, earning him purrs. "It's an honor to help you when stories about you have given me so much comfort when I'm stuck in the palace."

"No matter how tonight goes, you have my word I will help you escape from that awful cage." I shifted into my human form to convey the depths of my sincerity. "You are too good to be trapped in a place where no one appreciates you. Perhaps after your

Coming of Age ceremony, the time will be right to break you free."

"That would be amazing! I'm already dreading that stupid ceremony. If the people didn't expect it, my parents probably wouldn't bother."

"We shall make plans for later. But first, I need to take care of something before you can go on your fun adventure." I turned invisible in front of him, causing him to marvel at me. "I'll keep watch, so you have nothing to fear while you are out on the town. Live your night up to the fullest. We'll talk soon."

With that, I quickly made my way to the king's private bedchambers. Even in a plain tunic and britches, Rei looked entirely too royal, with his regal bearing and flame-red hair that was a dead giveaway that he was a member of the House of Hearts. "You call that a disguise?" I teased him as I appeared behind him in the mirror.

"Chess!" He spun around with a startled expression. "What are you doing here?"

"Come now, you can't possibly be surprised that I'm here. If you think I wasn't silently observing dinner, then you're more naïve than the young princeling."

A charming blush graced Rei's cheeks. "You shouldn't have been there!"

"No, but I'm very glad I was." I reached out and brushed his hair behind his ear. "I must admit, I'm stunned you agreed to his plan."

A hard edge came into Rei's gaze. "Did you put him up to this?"

"Shockingly, no. The scamp came up with that idea all by himself. But it's an idea worthy of this grand Cheshire cat." I embraced Rei, who stiffened for a moment before he hugged me back. "It means a lot that you want him to be right."

Rei held me tighter. "If he is, I'm going to feel like the dumbest fool in all of Wonderland. I'll surely be too stupid for you to want to be with after everything."

I pulled back to look down at him. "If you think anything could make me love you less, you don't know me as well as you claim." I cupped his cheek in my hand and brushed my thumb against it. "Every breath you take makes me love you more—even when you use it to say such silly things about me not being able to love you. There is no one who loves you more than me. Nothing will *ever* change that."

He dropped his gaze. "So, Prince Renner isn't your fated mate?"

"No, he's not. It's you." I leaned down to give him a tender kiss. "It's always been you."

"Then why didn't you tell me?" Rei demanded with a little heat in his voice.

I gave him a skeptical look. "Can you really stand there and swear you wouldn't have run the other way screaming if I told you in the beginning that fate brought us together and made you mine?"

He sighed as he covered my hand on his cheek with his. "I hate myself because the answer is 'no.' In the past, I would have rejected you and the notion that fate had any part in our relationship."

"And now?" I asked hopefully.

He held my gaze as he stroked the back of my hand. "If fate made you mine, then I want you to be *mine*. I'm so tired of running away from you, when all I want to do is stay."

My heart soared at his answer, which soothed my oldest fears. "I am yours, Rei. I always have been, and I always will be." When I kissed him again, it was with more heat.

"If you keep kissing me like that, I won't leave this room."

I chuckled at his threat. "Normally, that would be my goal, but this is the one time I want you to go away and do what you must. But before you go, I need to do one thing."

"What's that?"

I reached out and brought his beautiful red hair to my lips to kiss. I breathed magic into his hair, turning it into a dark shade of indigo to disguise him properly. As it worked its way from the tips to the root, it took hold in his eyebrows and changed his ruby-red eyes to match. "Mm, my midnight king. You look most bewitching at this hour."

Rei turned to look in the mirror and gasped at his reflection. He ran his fingers through his hair, as if he didn't believe what he was seeing. "Your magic never fails to astound me. Thanks, that will make it a *lot* easier to disguise myself."

"It sure will." I was pleased with my handiwork, although it was a tragedy to get rid of his coloring that was as fiery as him. "You'll have to lose that regal bearing on your own, though."

"When will the magic wear off?"

"Once you return to me at the palace." I embraced him from behind and met his gaze in the mirror. "You have it on my honor that I won't do a single thing tonight. Every word you hear tonight will be the truth, without any influence from me. I wouldn't jeopardize something this important, Rei."

He squeezed my arm. "I know."

I spun him around to face me once more, allowing me to press a tender kiss to his forehead.

"Now, go enjoy your night on the town with the young princeling and Zatinger. We will talk once you're returned."

Rei surprised me by stealing a last kiss before he left to meet them downstairs. I waited a few beats before I followed behind him in my invisible form. There wasn't a chance I was missing out on seeing all the fun happen.

But would the townspeople give him the answer he was hoping to find?

The potent smell of mead hit me as we entered the tavern near Zatinger's home. It was dim inside, with warm, low lighting in the wooden establishment that would help hide my identity. There was a lively crowd packing the enormous bar, filling the space with the sound of chatter and laughter. The place felt so alive compared to the silence at my palace. It was a little overwhelming.

"Come on, let's go grab a seat," Zatinger said as he guided me by the shoulder to head toward the rear of the seating area with Prince Renner at my side.

A woman in a low-cut red dress beckoned us over. "Hey, Zati! Bring your friends!"

"Ellezabeth, you're just the person I was hoping to see tonight," my bodyguard said as he gestured for me and Prince Renner to go over to her table. There were two other men with her, who were big, burly, and had more facial hair than I had ever grown in my entire life. They would have been intimidating if not for their rosy cheeks and big smiles.

"Oh, Mr. Midnight! Look at you! You're coming to sit next to me." She patted the seat beside her on the bench.

I looked at Zatinger, who tilted his head to indicate I should do as she asked. With a nod of acknowledgment, I sat down next to her. "Thank you."

"Well, well! It must be my lucky night." She wrapped her arm around my shoulder to tug me closer. "Hello, handsome! Where have you been all my life?"

Zatinger moved her off me as he sat on the other side of me, while Prince Renner settled across from us, next to one of the men. "Sorry, doll. He's already taken, so your efforts will be wasted. If you want someone to love all over, you'll have to settle for somebody else."

She turned her attention to the prince. "What about you, cutie? Has someone already had the good sense to claim you?"

Before he could answer, the big man sitting next

to him intervened. "Elleza, let these fine men drink in peace. Not everyone is here for your sexual pleasure."

She crossed her arms over her sizable bust. "You're planning on stealing him for yourself, aren't you?"

The man glanced down at Prince Renner, who stared at him with wide eyes. "Eh, he's a little young for my tastes. But give me a few more drinks, and we'll see how I feel later."

"I didn't bring them here for hookups, so all of you need to relax and let these men unwind in peace," Zatinger told them. "They're our newest recruits for the palace guard, so I'd appreciate you not chasing them off by being rude."

"Thank you for letting us join you this evening," I said. "I'm Reinard."

Ellezabeth squealed. "Ooh, look at the manners on this one. You're a right gentleman, aren't you? Are you sure I can't tempt you away from your lover? It's been such a long time since I've been with a decent guy."

The large man on the other side of the one sitting beside Prince Renner rolled his eyes. "I'll try not to take offense at that." He turned his attention to me. "I'm Narthaniel, Ellezabeth's sometimes fuckbuddy.

This guy next to me is Darrenth, her long-suffering brother. Nice to meet you both."

"Same here," Prince Renner said with a wave at everyone. "I'm Ariax. Heartsians really are as friendly as they say!"

"You're not from around here, are you?" Darrenth asked as he looked down at Prince Renner. "You sound like you're from Mirrorland with that accent."

Prince Renner rubbed the back of his head with a laugh. "Is it that obvious?"

Zatinger squeezed my shoulder to get my attention. "I'll go get some drinks."

"Thank you." I reached for my wallet, but he shook his head before walking away.

"So, why does a young kid from another kingdom want to defend our king?" Narthaniel asked.

"It'll probably make you laugh at how idealistic it is, but it's honestly because I really admire him. Unlike in my kingdom, King Rei works hard to make a difference for his people. He wants to make things better for everyone and not just maintain the status quo like in Mirrorland. I may not be able to do much, but I want to help him in any way I can."

Although his reasoning was a lie, I heard the truth in the prince's words. His kindness touched my heart in a way that once again made my guilt flare at not being able to be the man for him I should have been.

Darrenth ruffled Prince Renner's hair. "What a good lad you are, Ariax. It's nice to know that word of our wonderful king has spread even to Mirrorland."

"It's amazing what a difference it makes having a ruler who gives a damn about us common folk," Narthaniel said. "I had my suspicions about him when he first took the throne, but damned if he didn't prove us all wrong for doubting him."

Ellezabeth turned her nose up. "Hmph! Speak for yourself. *Some* of us had no qualms and knew from the very beginning that he would be an incredible ruler."

He arched a skeptical eyebrow at her. "I believe that has more to do with the fact you thought he was the most fuckable of the three brothers and, I quote, 'I wouldn't mind serving under him, if you know what I mean.'" He winked for good measure, making everyone laugh again.

She shrugged as she took a drink. "I stand by that statement. He's a king worth getting on your knees for. Someone better be sucking Our Majesty's glorious cock to reward him for all his selflessness. And why not me?"

I could feel my cheeks heating at her bawdy statements. But the situation became even more awkward for me as Darrenth said, "I hate to break it to you, but from everything I've heard, the only way our king would be interested in having a queen is if it's a man in drag."

"I know, but a girl can dream, can't she?" She rested her chin on her palm as she heaved a heavy sigh. "Why couldn't there be room for me in their threesome? I'm not opposed to wearing a strap-on."

Darrenth face-palmed as Narthaniel burst into laughter. I prayed my cheeks weren't on fire. Zatinger returned with a round of drinks for the three of us and asked, "What did I miss?"

"Elleza fantasizing about joining the king and the Cheshire cat in a threesome," Narthaniel said with a snicker. "But that's not news when she brings it up *every* time she's had two meads or more."

Prince Renner took a sip of his drink and coughed. His eyes watered as he said, "Wow, that's much stronger than the ale at home!"

Darrenth patted his back. "That's not a bad thing. Maybe it'll put some hair on your chest, boy."

The young royal's cheeks flushed. "I guess we'll find out." He took another sip before leaning forward with interest. "So, have you ever seen the Cheshire cat before?"

"Pfft, only in her dreams every night," Narthaniel scoffed, making everyone laugh again. I chuckled to fit in before taking a big swig of mead, but something deep inside of me stirred with jealousy. Rather than address the root of the issue, it was easier to blame it on the alcohol being much stronger than the wine at the palace.

"And when she makes you dress up as him when you role-play," Darrenth retorted, making Narthaniel groan. "As her brother, I did *not* need to know that about you two."

Narthaniel defended himself. "Hey, you found the cat ears and striped tail butt plug when you were snooping. You shouldn't have asked questions when you weren't ready to hear the answers."

"Wait, are you serious?" Prince Renner asked with wide eyes.

"You can't make this shit up. The tail plug even vibrates," Narthaniel replied, causing the young royal's mouth to drop open in a small O shape. "It feels good enough that I don't complain whenever she's feeling frisky for some feline fun."

I couldn't process the idea that people would enjoy sexual role-playing as Cheshire. While I tried to come to terms with that disturbing piece of knowl-edge, Prince Renner asked a question I wasn't expecting. "Wait, so if he's Cheshire, does that mean you dress up like the King of Hearts?"

"Of course! I even have a crown." She blew a kiss at Prince Renner, making him blush hard as I reeled from the information overload. It caused my mead to disappear faster than normal. "I quite enjoy making him bow down and kiss my ring, if you catch my drift."

"But don't you fear the Cheshire cat?" I asked once I could find my voice.

She snorted in a very undignified way. "Fear him? Baby, I want to fuck him. And despite what Narthaniel claims, he'd let that gorgeous god of a shifter fuck him if he had the chance." Everyone laughed as her partner huffed in annoyance. "I bet he'd even ask Cheshire to keep his ears and tail in his human form because he's a pervert, just like me."

"Only because you've corrupted me!" Narthaniel protested. "You filled my head with curiosity about what it would be like for a shifter to use their magic on me during sex."

It took effort not to let my mind drift to memories of all the ways Cheshire had used his powers on me in the bedroom. Those thoughts I couldn't afford to have with so many people around. I took another drink instead.

"If we're lucky enough, hopefully, we'll find out someday," she said with a dreamy sigh. I stiffened when she turned her attention to me. "What about you, Reinard? You're being awfully quiet about this conversation."

"Sorry, I'm just surprised. I always thought Cheshire was seen as a fearsome beast."

"Fearsome beast in bed, maybe." She laughed at her own joke. "Nah, the only people left who fear him are the asshole aristocrats, despite the former Queen of Hearts' best attempts to turn the common people against the good ol' Cheshire cat. But we're smarter than that. May her soul rest in the seventh layer of the Hearts of Hell forever."

"I'll drink to that," Zatinger said as he lifted his mug in a toast before taking a sip. "I'd happily take care of His Majesty for three eternities before serving one more cursed day under that she-demon."

His words didn't upset me. Not when I knew the hell my mother had put him through when he served in her royal guard. He had been part of the resistance that had dethroned her, which was the very reason I'd hired him as my personal bodyguard. His bravery had freed us all, even if it led to the unwanted result of me becoming king.

Darrenth raised his mug before calling out in a

loud voice that carried over the noise, "Long live our king!"

It stunned me when all the patrons stopped their conversations to echo his words and raise a glass to me. It filled my heart with warmth to see the towns-people show such support for me. Having them do it while unaware of my presence felt very different from when they were obligated to cheer for me at a formal event.

Ellezabeth wiped her mouth with the back of her hand when she finished her drink. "That man is the best thing to ever happen to this king-dom. And I'll personally break the nuts of the advisor who is making him so miserable by keeping him apart from Cheshire. His Majesty deserves to be as happy as he makes the rest of us."

I was too tongue-tied to speak, so Prince Renner took the lead. "People are still suspicious of shifters in Mirrorland, although they returned with the magic. Do you think everyone would support King Rei taking the infamous Cheshire cat shifter as a consort? I mean, his antics are pretty notorious to reach our kingdom."

"Let's take a poll." Zatinger stunned me when he got up on his bench with his mug of mead. "Is there anyone here who wouldn't drink to Our Majesty marrying the shifter known as the Cheshire cat?"

A stout woman at the bar stood with a slight sway. "Yeah, because he should marry *me*!" Her protest earned her a loud cacophony of boos that stunned me. She made a rude gesture with her fingers. "Ahh, fuck off! The king should be so lucky!"

Another woman in the audience booed her again. "Lucky to never lay eyes on you, maybe!" She stood up and raised her glass. "Three cheers for Queen Cheshire! Long may he reign in love and lust with our beautiful king!"

I was unprepared for the bellows of support from everyone in the tavern before they drank to my lover. I had always prided myself on being attuned to my people, but somehow, I had completely missed the mark with their opinion on Cheshire. How could I have gotten it so wrong?

Zatinger sat down again and gave my shoulder a squeeze before he leaned in to say words for my ears only. "His Majesty is very good at taking care of his people, but he's terrible about taking care of himself. After everything he's done, there isn't a single citizen who would begrudge him happiness with the one person who has stood by his side since the beginning. Hopefully, he can see that now."

I found it hard to speak around the lump in my throat. The revelations were staggering. I needed a moment to clear my head. "Sorry, I need to get some air. Stay with him."

"Only if you promise to stand in front of the window." He pointed at the one at the tavern entrance.

I nodded before I excused myself to go outside. The air was cool after being in the warm bar. I leaned against the glass with a shaky sigh, overwhelmed by what I had seen.

The door to the tavern opened, and I tensed when a man in a black cloak with a raised hood approached. But rather than danger, it was Bianco. He lowered his hood long enough to show Zatinger his face before putting it back up and grinning at me. "You've certainly learned a lot tonight, haven't you?"

"What are you doing here?"

"Alistair was working with Hatter and March with their donation drive, so his reward was a late-night tea party with them," Bianco said. I had made Alistair the official Alice Ambassador for the Kingdom of Hearts. He helped with goodwill and charity causes, like Hatter's company taking the left-over scraps of their fabrics to make clothes for the commoners that they gave away to the community for free.

Still reeling from everything, I didn't share in his good humor. "How did I get this so wrong, Bianco? How could I be *that* out of touch with my people?"

His expression softened. "You weren't always wrong. When you first took the throne, they feared that you would have a bloodthirsty dynasty like your mother. Announcing Cheshire as your consort back then would have caused an uproar. But when you have spent every moment of your reign these past few years doing everything in your power to take care of your citizens, you've earned their trust. And he will surely charm the few who may be against him at first."

"How will he ever be able to forgive me for what I've put him through the last three years?" Guilt ate away at me. "For all those times I've rejected him in the crown's name?"

"Because he loves you. And as painful as it was to be separated from you, we both know he enjoyed being able to chase you again, just like he did at the beginning of your relationship. Telling him no always makes him twice as determined to make you say yes."

I stiffened in surprise when Cheshire embraced me from behind in his invisible form. "Chasing you is fun, but catching you is the best," he whispered in my ear. He trailed kisses up my neck, sending a shiver through me. It was so daring, although no one could see him. "I forbid you from spending one more minute regretting the past. You can make it up to me when we return to the palace. Now, go back in there and keep talking to Ellezabeth. She's my new favorite person. Go have some guilt-free fun with her."

Bianco and I both laughed. I should have known her antics would entertain Cheshire. Since I couldn't interact with his invisible form without it looking weird, I settled for saying, "To be continued later."

"You can count on it, my love." He kissed my cheek before pushing me back to the door.

"Are you joining us?" I asked Bianco.

Bianco's hair changed to black as his eyes turned blue. The transformation was stunning. "Yes, because it'll be much more fun than eavesdropping from afar like before."

With my best friend at my side and my lover watching from his invisible vantage point, it was much easier to go back inside and rejoin the group.

Bianco lowered his hood when we approached the table. "Mind if I join the fun?"

"Not when you look like that, Mr. Tall, Dark, and Handsome," Ellezabeth said as she pushed her sizable breasts up higher, making the other men at the table groan. "What's your name, beautiful?"

He sat next to Prince Renner. "Conigli. It's a pleasure to make your acquaintance."

She tapped her lower lip. "Conigli? Are you related to the king's chief mage, Master Bianco?"

"Indeed. He's my cousin."

Her eyes lit up with delight. "Which means you're a rabbit shifter, too."

"I am."

"Ohhh, you better watch out, Narthaniel. She's going to have you wearing bunny ears and a vibrating cottontail next," Darrenth said, causing everyone to laugh as Narthaniel hid his face in his hand with a pained groan.

It felt good to laugh and feel the closest thing to carefree as I had been since taking the throne. It was so much fun; I might have to sneak out in disguise more often.

A few meads and hours later, I was warm and fuzzy in the best of ways as I headed back to the palace with Bianco, Prince Renner, and my bodyguard. Once I had overcome the enormity of my error in judgment, the evening had been fun. "Thank you for being such a great guide, Zatinger. I must say, your friends were quite spectacular."

"I'm grateful you have a sense of humor that can tolerate Ellezabeth's naughty mouth," he said with a chuckle. "I know she's bawdier than you're used to at the palace, but she means well."

"In truth, it was refreshing not being treated like a king for a night." The only person who had done that before was Cheshire.

Prince Renner had a bounce in his step. "That's the most fun I've *ever* had! Books really undersold how wonderful a tavern full of kind strangers could be."

It was a sentiment I understood well. "I'm glad you enjoyed yourself. Your father would kill me for corrupting you if he knew I took you out to rub elbows with the public, though."

"Maybe it's all the mead talking, but I don't care what he thinks. I'm tired of being a worthless sixth prince. Coming here was the best thing that's ever happened to me. And if Cheshire can't help me, then I'm making a run for it during the next marriage interview, especially if it's to that awful Princess of Diamonds my dad has his eye on."

I didn't have it in my heart to dissuade his desire to escape. From everything I had heard, it would be the best thing he could do. "Has Cheshire offered to help you?"

"Please don't get mad," Prince Renner pleaded as he looked up at me with wide seafoam-green eyes. "I met him in the forest on the way here earlier today. When he realized I was more interested in helping him get together with you, we combined forces."

I shook my head as we walked back to the castle, but it made me feel unsteady on my feet. "Why am I not surprised?"

"Because you know Cheshire," Bianco said wryly. "It's zero percent surprising."

Prince Renner hiccupped before he continued. "My original plan was to flirt with him to make you jealous, but I couldn't do that when I realized how much you loved him. I just wanted to help the two of you to be happy together. It's too sad that you've been kept apart."

"By my own stupidity, no less." I shook my head ruefully. "Even after my mother has been gone for years, she still finds ways to harm me."

"Living happily with him is the best revenge," Zatinger said. "I apologize if I overstepped earlier in the tavern with my comments about her."

I waved away his concern. "It's unnecessary. After everything she put you through, I understand your resentment of her. I certainly have no fondness for her. The only kindness she ever showed me was ignoring me for so long in favor of pouring all of her hatred into corrupting Rex." It felt weird to say my oldest brother's name after so many years. He was a memory I was happy to keep banished to the back corners of my mind.

"I'm glad you got to see tonight how much your people love you. You've become the great ruler this kingdom deserved. We are all indebted to your kindness and generosity. But you deserve to be happy, too," Zatinger said.

"This evening was definitely illuminating." Warmth bloomed in my heart as I remembered the townsfolk's reactions earlier. "I'm very grateful to have my eyes opened."

"Not to dampen the mood, but it must be addressed. Cheshire, forgive me for saying this, but your bonding will have to wait a few days," Bianco announced in an apologetic tone.

He materialized in his cat form, floating in front of us with a cross expression. "And what reason do you have that I would care about giving priority to over our long-awaited moment?"

"When you bond, you will be holed up for days as you indulge in your new connection," Bianco explained. "You need to give me time to arrange King Rei's calendar to allow for such a break. I didn't think to do that when I bonded with Alistair, and it caused some havoc."

Cheshire's tail flicked as he continued to float ahead of us while we walked. "This is not what I want to hear."

"You can still indulge in each other, but please give me some time to create the space for your bonding," Bianco requested. "You've waited a long time, and you deserve to not have it rushed because the king has too many important meetings coming up to miss."

Cheshire harrumphed. "You're lucky I love you both."

"Does that mean you'll wait a little while longer?"

"Yes, if only so I can continue to enjoy the young princeling's time while he is here." He floated over to perch on Prince Renner's shoulder, who reached up to pet him. "We have much to discuss before he leaves."

"Like how you're going to help me escape the palace once I'm back home?" Prince Renner asked hopefully. "Because I don't want to go back at all, but

I don't want King Rei to get in trouble with my father if I disappear while I'm here."

"I appreciate your consideration," I said. "But should you wish for refuge in the future, you will always have sanctuary on my lands."

"Thank you." He reached up and pulled Cheshire into his arms to cuddle, rubbing his face against the cat's. "This really has been the best night ever!"

Cheshire purred as he nuzzled the prince back. "And the night's not over. There will be more fun before the sun rises."

It sounded like I was in for a wonderful evening, even if we couldn't formally forge a mating bond yet. But there were plenty of other things we could do to entertain ourselves in the meantime.

ELEVEN

CHESHIRE

Upon returning to the palace, Rei and I were finally left alone in his room. He enveloped me in a crushing hug, allowing me to feel him trembling as he whispered, "I'm sorry. I'm so, so sorry, Chess." There was a soft sob in his voice that broke my heart as I held him closer.

It was a good thing that Rei rarely drank mead. On the very rare occasion he overindulged in it, he tended to become maudlin. I rubbed his back as I tried to soothe him. "You have nothing to be sorry about. Don't ruin your wonderful night with feeling bad about things that don't matter."

He pulled back to look at me with a pained expression. It was strange looking into indigo eyes, which reminded me to undo the magic. "But it *does* matter," he insisted as his features returned to their normal fiery coloring. "I never should have—"

I cupped his face in my hands to make him focus on me. "Rei, listen to me. You didn't leave me because you didn't love me anymore. You did what you had to do for your kingdom. I have always understood that and never held it against you because I knew that one day, you'd be mine again. I just needed to be patient."

The corner of his mouth turned upward in a wry grin. "But you're the *worst* at being patient."

"Yes, so please appreciate that I have bided my time until now."

He looked down with shame. "I can't believe that I was such a fool to not realize that my mother—"

"Rei." I forced him to meet my gaze once more. "Do not let that awful she-devil steal one more moment of happiness from you. She took three years from us, and that's enough. It's time to get revenge by living happily ever after. Agreed?"

He melted into my embrace as he snuggled closer to me. "I love you so much, Chess. I hope you know that every time I had to say no, all I wanted to say was yes. You're all I've ever wanted. That's why she wanted to keep us apart. And I was the fool who let her hurt us."

I held in a sigh at his predictable return to morose

regret. "You are the only good thing that woman ever did in her bloody reign. And you've become a good and kind king despite her efforts. That's why you put your people first when it was necessary. But now, for once in your life, it's time to prioritize your happiness."

He nuzzled against me. "Nothing makes me happier than you."

"And that is why you shall have me."

Rei pulled back without letting go. His red eyes were a little unfocused as he studied me. "May I ask an impertinent question?"

I had to bite my lower lip to hold in a laugh. "I'll allow it."

"We've made love more times than there are stars in the skies, so why didn't a bond form between us like Bianco and Alistair?"

"Get into bed, and I'll tell you."

I couldn't hold in the chuckle at the way he drunkenly fumbled out of his boots and clothes before clambering into bed. A simple flick of my magic was enough to disrobe me before I joined him in bed. To my surprise, he curled around me for a cuddle, relaxing against me with a contented sigh. I was usually the one who wanted to be held.

While it wasn't the amorous reunion I had been

hoping for, it felt like heaven for him to want me near without rejecting me. "To answer your question, Vivalter forbade me from forming a mating bond with you until the time was right."

"How do you know when the time is right?" Rei asked through a yawn.

"Because my know-it-all older brother can see the future. He foretold that should we mate too soon, it would cause your death. And since you are the one thing I cannot live without, I had no choice but to wait."

"Why did he never tell me that?"

A hint of shame descended on me. "Because I was a coward who never told you that you were my fated mate out of fear I would lose you back then."

"What would have happened if you had ignored him?"

"If I had mated with you early in our courtship, your mother would have had your head over betraying her by choosing a 'dangerous menace' like me over her." I hugged him tighter when he winced at the reminder of her fondness for beheadings. "If I had done it toward the end of her reign, during Regan's brief one, or the start of yours, you would have been assassinated the same as the queen and Rex."

He was silent for a long moment. "Because people would have thought you were controlling me on the throne?"

I nodded. "You weren't wrong to choose the crown over me in the beginning. Everyone saw me as a threat then. But a lot has changed in those three years."

"But how did it change so much that they're sexually role-playing us?"

His question was too funny not to snicker at. "Because you are the great king who not only made life better for his citizens, but you are powerful enough to return the magic to Wonderland."

He toyed with the hair at my nape. "But that had nothing to do with me. That was all Alistair and Bianco."

"Who restored the magic in the name of love and their beloved king. If there was ever a sign that you're on the side of good, it's bringing the light magic back to Wonderland and eradicating the darkness once and for all. Alistair-Once-Alice and Bianco are creatures made of magic, who brought only good into this realm. I could convince even the most suspicious of citizens that I am associated with the right side."

"Because you only mess with the aristocrats that they hate?"

I stroked his hair, relishing in his lack of rejection. "That, too. And I've been careful to be a good boy lately so I wouldn't cause you more trouble."

"It's funny. I should be mad at you and Prince Renner for teaming up against me, but I can't find it within me to get upset about it. He's a good kid." Rei sighed heavily. "Under different circumstances, he would have been an ideal consort. But I cannot love him the same way I live and breathe for you. He's more like the little brother I wish to protect."

My heart swelled at his romantic declaration. "As fond as I have become of the young princeling, I'm very glad to hear that."

"Are you really going to help him escape later?"

"That depends. Are you planning on telling me not to do it?"

He cuddled closer to me. "That's what I *should* do. But he deserves a better life. I want him to have what we have. And he can never have that as long as his parents are using him as a pawn to arrange alliances through a loveless marriage to someone as awful as the Princess of Diamonds."

"Prince Renner is destined for a great love like ours."

Rei chuckled. "Are you just saying that, or has your brother told you something?"

"The little princeling has a fated mate he has yet to meet."

"Ahhh, that's right. You asked Vivalter if Prince Renner would have his happily ever after this afternoon. I almost forgot." He hid a yawn. "So much has happened that today has felt like a year."

"You're not wrong." I pressed a kiss to his forehead. "Get some sleep, my love."

"But we didn't..." Rei trailed off, but I could feel the heated flush of his cheek against my chest that betrayed where his mind had gone.

I chuckled. "As much as I would love to make up for lost time and ravish you, it has been an eventful day, and you're still somewhat drunk. My ego couldn't handle you falling asleep in the middle of things."

He snorted in amusement. "I'm quite confident you could keep my interest aroused."

"Yes, but when I'm this tired and my beast knows you're *finally* allowed to be ours, I don't trust him not to take advantage of my lowered defenses." While my beast and I were normally in accordance with each other, it was the one circumstance where I feared he would overrule my common sense. "As much as I hate to admit it, Bianco is right. You don't have the luxury of saying the hell with it and doing what you want, whenever you want to. So, I will wait a little longer."

"I've missed your beast," Rei said, but his voice was getting fainter. "But I've missed you more."

As he drifted to sleep, I healed him from the hellish hangover he would otherwise have in the morning. More than anyone, he deserved a fun night without consequences. "We will have our moment soon. I can promise you that."

"We have six minutes."

I opened my eyes to find Rei straddled over me, gloriously naked and hard. "Good morning, gorgeous."

"Six minutes, Chess," Rei said insistently. "Then Bianco will be here to make me start my day. *Please*."

I tugged him down for a rough kiss as my magic slicked both of our cocks before working them together in tandem. That freed both my hands to caress him all over as I took special care to trail my claws against his skin. It resulted in him urgently rocking against me with the most delightfully needy noises.

"I need more than a few minutes," he groaned as his body moved in search of more pleasure.

"Not if I do this." I used my magic to penetrate him, taking great delight in manipulating that spot inside of him that made him orgasm every time I played with it. Today was no exception as he climaxed all over my stomach with a soft cry. "See?"

He playfully shoved my arm. "That wasn't supposed to be a challenge, show-off. I meant I want more than a quick frot with you." He leaned down and gave me a passionate kiss that I savored before he surprised me by reaching down to wrap his hand around my prick to stroke it. "I want *you* inside of me, not just your magic."

My beast stirred in its cage, more than ready to satisfy our mate's request. But after three years of foreplay building up, I refused to be satisfied with a quick rut. My voice came out in a dark growl. "Tonight."

"I'm holding you to that." All it took was Rei playfully nipping at my lower lip for me to come all over his hand. My beast once again threatened to come to the surface when Rei licked the cum off it while looking down at me. "*Both* of you, as a matter of fact."

Before I could respond, Bianco knocked on the

bedroom door. "Good morning, Your Majesty. May I come in?"

It was a crime to use my magic to clean us both and put on clothes, but I owed my king his dignity —even if I knew Bianco could smell what we had been up to. But the king didn't need to know that. As a final touch, I styled Rei's hair with a few braids.

He arched an eyebrow at me. "Is there some reason you're trying to make me pretty?"

"Because you're beautiful to me." I gave him a quick kiss before letting our friend in with an overly formal bow. "Good morning, most honorable Master Bianco. Won't you please join us?"

His nose flared slightly as he scented our activities, making me hide a grin behind my hand. "I'm impressed you're out of bed and dressed. I fully expected I'd have to turn on the hose to get you away from the king."

"Ha, I'd like to see you try." I scoffed, even though I wouldn't put it past Bianco to use his magic in such a way. "I'm being a good boy so he can be all mine tonight."

"As a reward, I'll give Your Majesty a later start tomorrow. Something tells me you'll need it." He smirked as Rei's cheeks turned pink.

The king cleared his throat. "It's appreciated. What do I have this morning?"

"First, you'll have breakfast with me, Alistair, and Prince Renner. Afterward, you and the prince will both be seeing Hatter, but you'll have to leave early for a meeting with your minister of finance about your plans to lower property taxes."

"Will my dear brother be joining them?" I asked.

Bianco shook his head. "I'm not sure. Much like you, Vivalter comes and goes as he pleases, with very little warning either way."

"Well, we *are* brothers. It's to be expected." I waved my tail behind me in amusement. "In that case, I shall also attend."

Bianco's gaze shifted to Rei, who nodded. "It's fine. As long as he behaves, he is welcome to stay."

It was a very good thing Rei didn't specify *how* I had to behave. That would make it even more fun later.

CHAPTER

TWELVE

REI

I t was amazing what a difference making the right decision about Cheshire did for my mood. I hadn't been jovial in a long time, but with the greatest love of my life sitting beside me at breakfast, how could I be anything but? It was the best kind of heaven not having to push him away anymore.

Prince Renner entered with an owlish squint, looking miserable, as he bowed before taking a seat at the table. "Good morning, Your Majesty and Cheshire."

"Are you unwell?" I asked.

He rubbed his temple with a wince. "My apologies. The mead last night was far stronger than the ale I'm used to back home. I don't drink very often, so I apparently have very little tolerance for it."

"My poor princeling," Cheshire said with a sympathetic tut. He gestured at the young royal's glass of boroberry juice, which swirled as it turned from a light blue to a shimmering purple. "There, that will help."

Prince Renner picked up his drink and marveled at the change. "That's amazing! What did you do?"

"I gave it a little boost of magic to help restore you to good health."

He lifted his glass. "I appreciate it." He didn't stop drinking it until he finished it all. A shiver passed through him as Cheshire's gift worked its magic. After a moment, he heaved a sigh of relief. "Oh, thank you. My head doesn't feel like it's being used for the royal marching band's drum practice anymore."

Bianco and Alistair entered my dining room, the latter with a wave. "Hi, Prince Renner! I'm Alistair!"

"It's an honor to meet you," the young royal replied. He looked at Alistair with awe.

"My apologies for the delay," Bianco said as he took a seat on my other side. "*Someone* didn't wish to get out of bed this morning."

"It's me. I'm that someone," Alistair said with

pride, making everyone laugh. "But in my defense, after a late-night tea party with Hatter, Vivalter, and March, who wants to get up early?"

I chuckled at his dilemma. "Yes, the morning always comes too soon after one of those types of evenings with them." I knew all too well from personal experience.

"Thus, you understand why he required a little extra coaxing this morning to get out of bed," Bianco said in an amused tone.

Cheshire grinned at him. "Something tells me he didn't object to your sensual wake-up call to entice him into *getting up*."

The innuendo in his tone brought a blush to Alistair's cheeks. But Bianco was unflappable as he retorted, "You say as if your morning was any different."

"It is a great pleasure to help His Majesty rise and shine." Cheshire's cheeky grin flustered me, especially when combined with Bianco's knowing smirk and Alistair's poorly concealed snickering behind his hand. That would take some getting used to.

I cleared my throat and gestured for the servants to serve breakfast. "Speaking of Hatter and his entourage, I forgot to ask if March will be in attendance when meeting Prince Renner later today?"

Bianco nodded. "March will almost certainly be with him. Vivalter is anyone's guess."

"I can't imagine my dear brother missing out on meeting Prince Renner," Cheshire said as he helped himself to a scone. In true cat fashion, he took a generous helping of clotted cream with each bite. "He would never pass up a chance to bewilder someone with cryptic insights that are as clear as mud."

The young royal blinked in surprise. "The royal seer is your brother? How have I never heard that before?"

"In order to keep his reputation pristine, Vivalter hid our association from everyone outside of our small circle of friends." Cheshire said it as if it was no big deal, but it had always bothered him, despite understanding why it was necessary. "But since most people have forgotten that he was once a *cat*erpillar before becoming a butterfly, they don't associate his illustriousness with the troublesome Cheshire cat."

Prince Renner's sympathy was sincere. "I'm sorry. That must be terrible having him hide you."

"It was not a choice I would have made, but I understand his fears that people would assume I was using my brother to have undue influence over the king."

The prince's expression turned thoughtful. "Do

you think his stance will change once you're the king's consort?"

"That is an excellent question. I'm sure he'll have a list of excuses why we must continue to maintain secrecy, but it is still worth asking about later." Cheshire helped himself to another scone. "He'll probably have some terrible vision that will come true if he were to acknowledge my existence to the world at large."

"After hearing so much about them, I can't believe I'm meeting Hatter and the March Hare today!" His boyish enthusiasm was sweet. After his help with getting me to open my eyes, I was glad I could treat him to a gift from the most talented designer in all of Wonderland.

"I felt like I was meeting a celebrity the first time I was introduced to them," Alistair said as he reached for a croissant. "Hatter and March are really down-to-earth. You'll love them. Vivalter is on another planet somewhere else, though. It's a fun place to visit, but you'll definitely leave confused."

I chuckled at his apt comparison. "Agreed. I don't think I've ever had a conversation with Vivalter where I had more answers than questions at the end."

"He prides himself on that," Cheshire added. "But I cannot blame him for it when it is a family weakness to enjoy a good riddle. Although, I have grown far more direct over the years than he will ever learn to be."

"As a warning, if you stand too close to him, you *will* get a contact high." Alistair snorted in amusement. "I don't know what he smokes, but it is some seriously high-grade stuff."

"My brother claims it's Aziraphaleian herbs that are only grown on the peaks of Crowley's Cliffs."

Prince Renner's jaw dropped open in shock. "I thought that place was just a legend! They say that's where the demon fairies live. It's real?"

"Perhaps it is. It is certainly a good cover story for what his herbs actually are."

"What are they?"

Cheshire grinned broadly. "Why, catnip, of course!"

Alistair's shocked expression was comical. "Are you seriously telling me I was getting a contact high from *catnip*? How can a human be affected by that?"

"It's laced with fairy dust, which is the part you would be reacting to," Cheshire explained. "It also helps unlock his mind's eye to the future."

The savior of Wonderland shook his head in amazement. "You'd think I'd be used to it by now, but I will never stop being shocked by how wild things are here." He turned pensive as he ate a tart berry muffin. "But if Vivalter's a butterfly now, why would catnip work on him?"

"Because regardless of form, he is still a Dëvîlskātž at heart."

As the conversation continued, I observed the others while enjoying my breakfast. It amazed me how easily Alistair was able to befriend Prince Renner, despite it being their first meeting. He had an amazing ability to make any stranger feel like his best friend. It was what made him such a wonderful Alice Ambassador for the Kingdom of Hearts. His friendly charm soon won over the most distrusting commoner.

"Is everything well with Your Majesty?" Bianco asked as Alistair, Cheshire, and Prince Renner continued their riotous conversation.

For once, I didn't have to lie. "Never been better."

"It will be even more wonderful once you're mated."

The thought was almost unfathomable to me when I already felt like I had everything I needed. "That moment can't come soon enough."

Bianco bowed his head. "I am doing my utmost to make it happen sooner rather than later, Your Majesty. I only have a few more things to reschedule before you are free to find your happiness together at long last."

While Cheshire engaged in the conversation with the other two humans, his tail brushed against the back of my hand. Instead of pushing it away like I had been forced to for the past three years, I delighted in giving it teasing strokes. My reward was a playful look that promised he'd be returning the favor to another part of me that would very much enjoy that kind of attention.

I needed Bianco to clear my calendar as soon as possible. Because once I got Cheshire into bed, I had no intention of letting him go again. How much longer would I have to wait before he was my mate? And how had I waited so long to make that happen?

t wasn't hard to find Hatter on the road. His carriage was quite easy to find since it was made of purple teakwood with gilded accents. I popped inside and made myself comfortable on his lap in my cat form. "Good morning to you both!"

I loved that he always greeted me with a delighted smile. "My dearest Cheshire!" Hatter gave me a loving scritch behind the ears that made me purr. He was perpetually fashionable, but he looked particularly stylish in his turquoise three-piece suit and silver shirt and tie. Despite his name, he had forgone a hat today in favor of an impressive series of braids in his long teal hair. "What a pleasure to have you join us!"

I was surprised Vivalter wasn't with them. "Where is my wayward brother?"

Hatter shrugged. "He said he would attend when it was time and not a moment before. When that is, nobody but him knows."

"Are you on your way to cause mischief, or have you already been banned for the day?" March asked in an amused tone. He preferred more subtle looks and had opted for a black suit, shirt, and vest paired with a metallic gold jacquard tie. His brown hair was tied into a high ponytail, giving him an elegant air.

It was a fair question when I had been banished from the castle more times than I had toe beans. "Our Majesty has finally seen the errors of his ways. He will become my mate once Bianco can arrange his calendar to allow for it." I preened as they congratulated me.

Hatter fluffed up my mane. "Oh, what splendiferous news! I know these past three years have been so hard on you both." He gave me a fond kiss on the top of the head. "This is truly a frabjous occasion, my dear friend. My heart is so overjoyed for you both."

"Congratulations on finally out-stubborning the king," March said with a chuckle. "I'm impressed it only took three years. I figured he'd need at least five before he'd break."

In my lonelier moments, I had feared the same thing. I had never been so glad to be wrong. "While you were entertaining our beloved Alistair, I went to a tavern with the king, the prince, and the bodyguard. It was a most illuminating outing for both royals."

March chuckled. "I can only imagine what kind of tawdry things King Rei and Prince Renner heard there."

"There was a particularly bawdy madame who gave them both all kinds of an education." I snickered at the memory of Ellezabeth. "But it was to my great advantage, so it was worth having to watch all the fun from my invisible vantage point above them all."

"How did you get the king to agree to that? I can't imagine him willingly going to a commoner's tavern."

I grinned at the question. "The funniest part is it was the young princeling who came up with the plan, all on his own."

March tilted his head. "But if you're getting together, what happens to the marriage interview?"

"I count all my lucky stars that King Rei loves me too much to be wooed away from me." I nuzzled against Hatter in a bid for more pets, which he gladly gave me. "While I was prepared to hate the little princeling and make life tremendously difficult for him, he is too pure and sweet. In truth, he would have made an excellent consort and partner for Rei. If I wasn't aware that fate had made Rei mine, I might feel bad about standing between the two of them in a different circumstance."

"I am surprised to hear you say such kind things about young Prince Renner," Hatter said as he gave me a rub under the chin that was so satisfying I stretched into it.

I curled up in a ball on Hatter's comfortable lap. "He is all things good and kind. It would be annoying if he wasn't so likable."

"He must really be something for you to not have a bad word to say about him," March said with an interested hum. "What did he do to win you over?"

"At first, he offered to help sabotage the marriage interview to make Rei mine. But beyond that, he is a genuinely sweet boy who has lived a very sad and lonely life in the palace, with only servants for friends."

One of March's elegant eyebrows arched upward. "He's friends with them? Most princes wouldn't bother to learn the staff's names, let alone be that friendly with them."

"They entertain him by recounting all the rumors and gossip that they hear in town and when they travel to visit family. He's remarkably well-informed as a result." It still amazed me how much he had gathered from their word of mouth. "He dreams of a life of fun and adventure, but he can't have that when he's trapped behind the palace walls. And if that wicked Princess of Diamonds gets her hands on him, it would be worse than being ignored by his own family."

March winced sympathetically. "I've never heard a good story about that woman. I'm pretty sure she took the place of the most hated person in all of Wonderland after the former Queen of Hearts was assassinated. And his family wants to bind him to *her* of all people? I mean, sure, she's a princess, but they should at least have some standards. That old fool, the Archduke of Spades, would be better."

I sighed as I rested my chin on my paws. "He is but a pawn for his parents. They care not for his happiness. And I simply can't abide by that when he is kindness personified."

Hatter comforted me with soothing pets. "So, what is your plan?"

I lifted my head to look at him. "My plan?"

"When you can't abide by something, you always take action." Hatter gave me a fond smile. "So, what is your plan to free the poor prince from his gilded prison?"

"You know me so well." I purred with pleasure. "While I haven't come up with an idea quite yet, I'm sure it will be brilliant once I do."

"Should you require it, you'll have our assistance," Hatter promised.

March glanced at his boss in surprise. "You're offering before you meet Prince Renner?"

"Yes, because if he is a man who won over the heart of the stubborn Cheshire cat, who was ready to unleash chaos and mayhem on the boy, he must truly be something remarkable. Plus, as I would always do anything to help a friend, that offer also extends to a friend of my friend."

March tapped his chin as he pondered something. "I'm not sure how helpful we could be in breaking him out of the Mirrorland palace since we have no real connections there. But we could at the very least employ him to help him get on his feet before deciding where he wants to go next."

"That's the spirit!" Hatter brightly said. "This is why I leave you in charge of everything that requires forethought. You've already found a clever use for the boy."

March crossed his leg over his knee, so I reached out to bat at his shoelaces. "I'm not sure it's *that* clever, considering he's a prince who has never worked a day in his life and probably has no practical skills."

"But he can be taught," Hatter reminded him. "If he is willing, he will learn."

"I am confident that he would work hard to not let you down," I said. It was something I had the utmost faith in. "You have never met a more appreciative prince."

"I'm certainly looking forward to meeting him. This should be wonderful fun."

I purred as Hatter continued petting me. Having him and March helping would make it much easier to help Prince Renner break free.

Since I now had free rein of the palace, I rode on Hatter's shoulder in my cat form as he made his way to the meeting. It surprised me when March stayed with the carriage to talk to the servants. "Why isn't he coming with us?"

"Once he arranges the drop-off of today's shipment, he will join us anon." Hatter walked through the confusing maze of hallways with ease, carrying his large sketchbook under his arm. "It was more uniforms for the king's newest hires, so it shouldn't take him too long. Our designs from yesterday will take a few weeks before we're able to deliver them."

A servant let us into the room once we arrived. The king sat at the head of the table, with the prince on his right. Rei's expression turned amused at the sight of me riding high on Hatter's shoulder, but he didn't comment on it for a change. "Welcome, Hatter. I appreciate you coming here on such short notice."

"I am never too busy for my king," the designer said with a slight bow. Over the years, he had mastered the fine art of doing that while I perched on him. It always amazed me how he could say such smooth lines without it sounding overly fawning. "I also appreciate the chance to make Prince Renner's acquaintance. Thank you for the honor."

"The honor is all mine!" Prince Renner said in a rush of words. "I can't believe you're really here—and for me!"

"I shall see that you have the grandest outfit for a Coming of Age ceremony, worthy of a wonderful young prince becoming a man." Hatter sat down on the left of the king and opened his sketchpad. "What side of yourself do you wish to show to the world at that event?"

Prince Renner blinked several times. "Um, I'm

not really sure how to answer that? I usually do my best to hide when I'm back at home."

Hatter's gaze softened. "Understood. In that case, let's start with more basic questions and work our way up to the philosophical ones. Does that work for Your Highness?"

He nodded. "Yes, sorry."

I jumped off Hatter's shoulder and wandered over to Prince Renner to headbutt him on the arm. "There is no need to be sorry, silly boy."

He petted my head with a sigh. "Sorry, I really don't like being difficult."

Hatter chuckled heartily. "Oh, my dear boy. If that is you being difficult, we have nothing to worry about. What colors do you like?"

"Greens, purples, blues, mostly." In contrast to his preference, his current outfit was a simple white tunic with a subtle damasks print and silver trim. "They're not really a color, but I enjoy iridescent and metallic fabrics. But my parents think they're too flashy and ostentatious for the royal family to wear."

"Nonsense," Hatter declared with a dismissive wave of his hand. "A Coming of Age ceremony for a young prince is the exact time people expect a royal to look the part of a shining prince."

He shrugged. "I'm the sixth son and twelfth child,

so my parents aren't interested in investing more than they have to for this final ceremony. They're glad to *finally* be done with the hassle and expense of it all."

"Well, then it is a splendid thing that they won't be paying for this outfit. That means you can wear whatever you'd like." He began sketching framework lines for the body shape. "Forgive my candor, but their thinking is quite backward on the matter. Since you are the final child, your ceremony should be the grandest of all as the last one the people will see for a long time. They wish to celebrate with you, so it should be a fantabulous party for all."

"I find that hard to believe when most of them are barely aware I exist. Since I'm not of age yet, my older siblings take care of all the meet-and-greet public type of events. The general populace never really sees me except at the jubilee and holiday parades. And I stay out of the headlines since I rarely get to leave the palace."

"In that case, we shall make you unforgettable."

He rubbed the back of his head with a sheepish expression. "I'm not sure that's a great idea when I'm planning to escape."

"It's all the more reason. You'll be remembered as the brilliant one who got away. That's far better than being a forgettable Prince What's-his-name."

"You mean like my siblings three through eleven?" Prince Renner asked with a laugh.

There was a knock before Bianco entered the room with a bow. "Forgive the interruption, but it's time for Your Majesty to meet with your finance minister."

"Very well." King Rei stood to leave, so I walked over to the other end of the table by the door to wait for him. I curled my tail around me as I looked up at him as he passed. He hesitated for a moment before giving me a kiss on the forehead and a quick scruff scratch that made me purr. "I'll see you later tonight."

I licked his hand to give him kisses in my cat form. Even as a feline, the taste of my mate drove me wild. "I'll make sure of it."

After his departure, I walked over to his vacated chair and jumped down to sit on it. I shifted into my human body but kept my cat ears and tail.

"You weren't wrong before," Prince Renner told Hatter. "Outside of the heir and the spare, there's no interest in me or any of my siblings. It's the one thing that I've never understood about my parents."

"You mean why they don't pay attention to all twelve of you equally?"

The prince shook his head. "No, why they had so many of us. My parents are frugal and obsessed with having a reputation for an austere rule. But having twelve kids is a tremendous investment for anyone, even a royal family. They handed us off to a wet nurse and then nannies, so it wasn't that they enjoyed spending time with us as children. We're just there in the shadows, waiting to be married off. All I can figure is they were planning to have as many pawns as possible to make alliances in all the kingdoms in Wonderland and beyond."

Hatter's expression was sympathetic. "No wonder you wish to escape from such neglected obscurity. I can see why Cheshire has pledged to assist you in your quest to break free. You shall have my help as well."

The shock on Prince Renner's face was comical. "Really? But you just met me."

"Not only have you won over Cheshire and our great king, but your story is not unfamiliar to me. As someone who had to strike out on his own to make it in a harsh world a long, long time ago, I know the value of having friends who can help you out."

Tears welled up in his eyes as he bowed his head. "Thank you. That means a lot to me."

There was a knock on the door before March entered the room with a formal bow. "I'm sorry I'm —" March faltered in both steps and words when he drew closer to the table and saw the prince. It took a moment for him to recover his senses. "My apologies. I regret being late, but I was dropping off the shipment of new uniforms to the staff."

March sat down beside Prince Renner, which was a signal to me that my brother would be arriving before the meeting was over. His rabbit nose was working overtime with little flares as he drew in breaths.

I sniffed out of curiosity to see what he was smelling, but nothing was amiss. *Curiouser and curiouser.*

Whereas Prince Renner had a sense of awe when meeting Hatter, there was a sudden shyness as he introduced himself to March. "It's very nice to meet you, sir."

"The pleasure is all mine, Your Highness." March held the young royal's gaze for a long moment, with some unspoken sentiment echoing between them. You could almost feel the electric spark zinging between them. It was a most exciting development.

"As always, you have impeccable timing," Hatter told his assistant. "I was informing Prince Renner that should he wish it, he could come work for us when he forges his way into a brave new world of adventure."

"Really?" The excitement in Prince Renner's voice was obvious. "You would actually hire me, despite having no real work experience?"

"Through no fault of your own," March said. "But if you are willing to learn, we will train you."

"I'll do anything you want!" It took a moment for his words to sink in, and his cheeks grew bright red at the unintentional innuendo. "Uh, I mean do anything to help. I'm happy to learn how to do any job you assign me."

Before anyone could respond, a rainbow butterfly fluttered through the window into the room before he shifted into my brother. Vivalter was as shimmery as ever in lilac and silver robes that billowed behind him with an unnatural wind.

"*Wow*," Prince Renner breathed under his voice. I couldn't blame him for being so impressed with my ethereal sibling. Like me, Vivalter knew how to make a flashy entrance.

Vivalter bowed to the young royal. "A splenda-cious day to you all."

As he always did, Hatter looked at my brother with all the love in his heart. "You are a resplendent vision, Vivi." I would never understand why the two dunderfluffs had yet to mate when it was obvious how much they adored each other.

Vivalter walked over to sit next to Hatter, settling his robes with a grace few could manage. "After seeing you in visions, it is a delight to meet you in person, Your Highness."

The information seemed to stun Prince Renner. "You've seen visions about me?"

"Indeed, they have been more frequent of late. Fate has made many plans for you."

"I don't suppose you can tell me what those are?"

I chuckled at his innocent question. "The first thing you will learn about my older brother is nothing is ever that straightforward with him."

Vivalter ignored me and remained focused on the prince. "You would be wise to accept the help of everyone here. In particular, Hatter's plan to partner you with March will bring many marvelous things into your life."

I glared at my brother for proving me wrong before turning my attention back to Prince Renner. "The second thing you'll learn about him is that he loves to contradict people."

"We are one and the same, you and I," Vivalter reminded me. "Yet you say it with such disapproval."

"Partner with me specifically?" March asked, refocusing us on the discussion. "In what way?"

Vivalter shrugged. "That depends on what you think he's best suited for."

"You know I fret over how you take on too many responsibilities," Hatter told March. "Prince Renner would make a fine assistant to ease your burdens. Would that satisfy your visions, dear Vivi?"

He steepled his fingers as he studied the young royal. "It is indeed one path he may take to finding happiness and fulfillment in his future."

"What's the other path?" Prince Renner asked.

"It's too early to tell. But both will lead you to the place where you belong," Vivalter replied.

March watched my brother carefully. He knew it was the little inflections that told the most details. "Does it also involve me?"

"Perhaps."

"Under what circumstances would it involve me?" I had to hand it to March. He was far more tenacious about trying to get specific answers out of my brother than most.

"Choices that have yet to be made. But all will reveal itself in time."

Whereas my sibling's vagueness usually vexed people, Prince Renner looked relieved. "I can really escape?"

"Not only can you, but I would highly recommend that you do."

The young royal blanched. "What happens if I don't?"

I expected my brother to give his standard reply that a question like that is best left unanswered. To my surprise, he responded with details. "Your parents will take into consideration your failure during the marriage interview with King Rei, then decide it is more practical to unilaterally decide to marry you off to someone of their choosing than rely on you to close a deal."

"To whom?"

Once again, Vivalter stunned me by not dancing around the topic. "The Princess of Diamonds will make an offer your parents won't refuse. You will be trading one prison for a far worse one. It will set off a chain reaction of events that will lead Wonderland back to war once more."

"*War?*" Prince Renner repeated in disbelief. "How does her marrying *me* cause a war?"

I looked at my brother suspiciously. "And why are you being so generous with information for once?"

"Because after barely surviving the bloody reign of the former Queen of Hearts, I have no desire to suffer through Princess Yechelle becoming a dangerous queen who will be worse than her dead idol." His answer chilled me.

Prince Renner's upset was distressing. "But how am I the only thing standing in the way of a Wonderland war?"

"Part of her marriage contract with your parents is that they will give loyalty to her and cater to her every whim. Upon her ascent to the throne, Queen Yechelle demands their support for her invasion of the Kingdom of Spades, and they are forced to give it. King Rei won't abide by that and raises his allies to prevent the attack. The result is a bloody massacre, the likes of which haven't been seen since the Magic Wars."

"It'd be better that I never went home at all than let that happen!" Prince Renner's distress was palpable. I reached over with my tail to brush against the back of his hand in silent support.

Vivalter tilted his head with an indecisive noise. "That's not true, unfortunately."

"Will my parents blame King Rei for my disappearance and attack him?" Prince Renner petted my tail under the table. "Because that sounds like something my father would do to save face."

"For one so young, you are quite wise," Vivalter

said with a hint of rare approval in his tone. "That is indeed how that situation would play out."

The prince was silent as he reflected on all the distressing information. "But what happens with Princess Yechelle if I escape and refuse to marry her? Won't there be dire consequences?"

"There will be, but not for you." Vivalter's mouth turned up in a smirk. "She will make a critical misstep that will lead to her downfall and spare the lives of millions. You will be the unknown savior of Wonderland."

Prince Renner shook his head. "But how am *I* that important? I'm nobody special."

"I disagree. You are quite special, indeed." It was unusual praise coming from my brother. "More special than you realize. Great things await you, but timing is everything."

"So, if I run away too soon, there's war. If I stay too long, there's war. When is the right time to avoid the worst-case scenario from occurring?"

"There will be an unmistakable moment that will tell you it is time for you to depart. Rest assured, you will know when you know."

"Ahh, there's that clear as Lake Wibbly Bibbly mud vagueness that you're so infamous for," I teased my brother.

He pointedly ignored me. "We all have a part to play."

"But why is my role so big when I don't matter?"

"Because you *do* matter, to a great number of people, actually," Vivalter corrected him.

Prince Renner rubbed his temples. "This is so much to take in and process! How can *I* be literally the only thing standing between all-out war?"

"Because fate is confident that you will make the right choice, whereas others would falter."

"Dearest Vivi, would you indulge my curiosity?" Hatter asked.

My brother's gaze softened. "You know I can deny you nothing." When I snorted at the ridiculous claim, Vivalter shot me a dirty look.

I held up my hands defensively. "What? If you couldn't deny him anything, you would be mated already."

"Vivi's reasons to delay are his own." It didn't escape my attention that Hatter reached under the table to hold my brother's hand. "What brings about the downfall of the wicked Princess of Diamonds after Prince Renner makes the right choice?"

When Vivalter didn't answer immediately, I couldn't resist goading him. "You know you want to tell us. It's no fun when you're the only one who knows what will happen."

To my surprise, he relented. "She makes the critical mistake of setting her sights on the third Princess of Clubs."

"Princess Kathalia?" Prince Renner asked. "I've met her a few times. She's one of the very few royals who has been genuinely nice to me. We still exchange letters sometimes."

"Her soul is kindred to yours, and you would do well to remember that in the future. She has a gentle spirit but a spine of steel and a heart full of righteousness for fairness and justice for all. When fate calls on her to play her part, she will do it perfectly."

"What happens to her?" Prince Renner asked in a worried tone.

"She will sacrifice herself for her family by marrying that heartless woman."

"No!" Prince Renner's distress made me once again brush my tail against his hand. "Princess Kathalia shouldn't have to do that!"

"With a wife at her side, Princess Yechelle will have her parents assassinated in order to take the throne."

An icy chill of dread ran through me at the thought of what atrocities that woman would be capable of as queen. "But wouldn't that mean war would happen, anyway?"

Vivalter hesitated before he continued. "No. Kathalia will discover her wife's plans and put an end to it once and for all by revealing the truth to their people. In doing so, the evil queen will be vanquished, and Queen Kathalia will have a long and prosperous rule. She will become close allies with King Rei, and the people of both kingdoms will benefit from their flourishing alliance built on the same values and ideals. Wonderland will know only peace, thanks to Princess Kathalia's sacrifice. I can assure you she will be well rewarded for her efforts."

Prince Renner reeled at the flood of information. "Princess Kathalia will make a great queen, but what an awful thing to suffer through in order to reach that point."

"She will consider it a worthy sacrifice and won't have any regrets." Vivalter held the prince's gaze. "You cannot warn her. It will throw everything into chaos should you do so."

He bowed his head. "I understand."

"Knowing the future can be both a great relief and a heavy burden to bear. But it is important that you know all of this, so you can make the correct decisions."

Prince Renner was silent for a moment. "Because I would have tried to talk Princess Kathalia out of marrying the Princess Yechelle when I found out about the engagement."

"And you would have been successful, with the blood of millions on your hands." Vivalter's tone softened. "That is a burden I know you could not bear. So be forewarned and forearmed, but keep this a secret for your consolation only. Fate will do what it must."

The young royal looked at Vivalter with curiosity. "How do you live with knowing how many horrible things could be happening?"

"By playing my part to help those in need of such guidance make the right choices."

"Thank you for telling me." Prince Renner drew a shaky breath. "I promise I'll take everything you said to heart."

March searched my brother's gaze for something. "And what happens when he comes to work for me?"

Vivalter's smile was enigmatic. "That is a surprise I have no intention of ruining."

I noticed the hare shifter's nose flaring softly again. He seemed unsettled by something, and I was dying to know what was causing his unease.

"Well, that's enough heaviness for one afternoon," Hatter declared. "Let us focus on something with far lower stakes. Prince Renner, what clothing style do you most admire? I know Ventruvian high-collars are all the rage in Mirrorland right now."

As the young royal began to answer, March abruptly excused himself. I waited a few moments before I got up to follow him, my curiosity burning about what had gotten into him.

I found March pacing down another hallway, which was most unlike him. He was always cool and level-headed under any type of pressure or situation. "What has unsettled you so, my friend?"

He froze as he looked at me, then sighed heavily as he ran a hand through his brown hair. "Sorry, I just needed a minute to breathe and clear my head."

I thought back over the conversation. March had been quiet during all the talk of war and consequences. He only seemed concerned about the prince being made his partner. That's when it connected for me. "Oh, I see."

He crossed his arms over his chest. "See what?"

"You needed to breathe air in a room without a certain princeling by his side." I couldn't stop myself from grinning when I saw a flash in his eyes of his beast momentarily breaking through to the surface. It had been a *very* long time since I had gotten a glimpse of him. "It seems he has stirred your beast."

"That shouldn't happen!" March flinched at the harshness of his tone. "Sorry."

"What issue do you have with the prince?"

March shrugged. "I have no business getting involved with any member of a royal family."

"Yes, but Renner is a prince who wishes to be a pauper, which is quite a separate thing, you know." My grin turned to a smirk. "Especially when he seems so eager to serve under you and learn to do whatever you want him to."

March's beast resurfaced. "Do not mock us, cat. We are in no mood for your antics."

"Of course you aren't. I'm not nearly as much fun as pinning that pretty princeling against that table and mating him."

His beast tried to throw me against the wall, but my cat reflexes made it easy to dodge his grasps. "Why are you provoking us?" I could see the ripple of rage run through him. "And why can I smell him on you?"

"Because I have it on good authority from my brother that Prince Renner is destined to have a happily ever after with his fated mate. And given that I've never seen you lose your cool in all the hundreds of years of our friendship, it's not difficult to connect the dots when your beast is growling at me for having Prince Renner's scent on me."

March reached up to hold his temples as he closed his eyes with a shuddering sigh. He took a few moments before he opened his eyes and returned to normal. "My apologies. I am unaccustomed to my beast being so unruly."

"No apologies are necessary. It's quite fun, actually." I waved my tail with excitement.

"Not from this side." March frowned as he took a few steps back from me. "That boy is too young, too royal, and too in need of help for me to put him in that situation. My beast must be wrong."

I snorted at his stupidity. "Do you really believe that after hearing my brother talking about Prince Renner 'partnering' with you?"

He sighed heavily. "It does not bode well for me."

"Why do you say that?"

"Because even if he is my fated mate, I cannot act on it when he must return home until some undetermined point in time when he can finally return to my side." A shiver ran through him as he had another internal bout with his beast. "I've only been by his side for less than an hour, and already the thought of such distance between us is agony. How could you bear being apart from King Rei for *years*? How do your brother and Hatter live so close without being together?"

I shook my head at his latter question. "If you can figure out the answer to that, you'll be the smartest person in all of Wonderland."

"What in the seven hearts of Hell do I do now?"

I held March by the shoulders and gave him a supportive squeeze. "You go in there, act like everything is fine, and get to know the young princeling. Luckily for you, to know him is to love him." March's eyes flashed with his beast's jealousy, but he held him at bay. "You're a lucky man, March. And something tells me you won't have to wait as long as you think."

His expression turned remorseful. "Forgive me, old friend. I did not mean for my beast to react to you in such a shameful way."

I hugged March. "There is nothing to forgive. Your beast will calm in time. Besides, it is not as if I am any stranger to mine taking over with Rei."

"I'm honestly amazed you're listening to Bianco and not locking the king up in his tower until he's too exhausted to move." March chuckled as he began walking back to the room.

"Even my beast can see the rationale behind his logic. We have waited a long time for this moment. A few more days is not so hard when I know he's willing to finally be mine in every sense of our mating bond."

Before we entered the room, March hesitated. "Thank you for talking some sense into me."

"You're welcome. Enjoy your new adventure." It would be exciting to watch from the sidelines.

We both returned to the room to our seats. Hatter's expression was full of concern. "Is everything well?"

"Yes, I just needed to pass a note to a servant to deliver to the staff regarding something I forgot to mention with the uniforms," March replied, the picture of unflappable calmness once more.

"And you know me, I have to put my nose in everything," I said with a cheeky grin.

"Well, you're back just in time to help take Prince Renner's measurements."

It was hard to smother my chuckle at March's wide eye stare at his boss. He cleared his throat as he regained control of himself. "Of course."

"As entertaining as this is, I am needed elsewhere," Vivalter announced. "Be strong, Prince Renner. Good things will be coming your way. March, Hatter, I'll see you later this evening."

Hatter captured my brother's hand before he

walked away, bringing it to his lips to kiss. "I eagerly await our reunion, my beloved Vivi."

Vivalter brushed his thumb against Hatter's hand holding his. "As do I." With that, my brother shifted into his rainbow butterfly form and floated out the window.

Prince Renner shook his head in amazement. "Is he always so...that?"

Hatter chuckled. "Yes, Vivi is always a majestic creature of such wonder and splendor."

"That's one way to describe him," I said with a snort.

Hatter ignored my comment and gestured for Prince Renner to move to the empty corner of the room that had more space. "Please stand over there so March can take your measurements."

"If I may, Your Highness?" March asked in a soft voice as he stood before the shorter prince.

It was endearing seeing how shyly the younger man reacted. "Yes, please. Thank you."

I took enormous delight in watching March stand before the prince, doing his best to stay professional as he called out the measurements for Hatter to mark on his sketch. But I could see the tremble in the rabbit shifter's hand and the shivers that ran through him every time he touched the prince. By the time

March lowered to his knees, Prince Renner's cheeks were a charming shade of pink.

I had a great deal of sympathy for how hard March was struggling to keep his beast at bay while at the perfect height to pleasure his newly discovered fated mate. His fight became even harder when Prince Renner murmured, "Your green eyes are so beautiful."

"I'm gratified you think so," March replied, but I could hear that rumble of his beast threatening to take hold.

Like a man in a trance, Prince Renner ran his fingers through March's brown hair while looking down into his eyes. "It's as soft as bunny fur," he whispered in awe before he realized what he had done. He pulled his hand back as if he had been burned. "I'm so sorry! I don't know why I did that!"

It was a mystery to him, but I knew why. Even without being a shifter, something deep within Prince Renner reacted to his future mate. Hatter was about to say something to them, but I shook my head to stop him.

"It's okay," March told him in a soothing voice. "I don't mind."

The prince's blush reached all the way to the tips

of his ears. "I'm sorry, I wasn't trying to be disrespectful. It just looked so soft. I was compelled to touch it."

"I truly don't mind." March's lips turned up into a smirk as he measured the inseam of Prince Renner's leg, earning him a cute gasp. It was too precious watching the young man trying not to react to their close positioning. "A little curiosity never hurt anyone."

"But it was rude of me!"

March took the measurements for the other leg. "It's only rude if I object." Having finished, he stood up and towered over the shorter man. "And I certainly have no objections."

Once again, I could feel their connection almost sparking as they stared deep into each other's eyes. But Hatter shattered the moment when he announced, "Wonderful! I believe we have everything we need. We'll get started on this immediately, and once it's ready, we'll have you to the atelier for a fitting in a few weeks."

Prince Renner reached up to feel his cheeks. "Thank you. For this, and everything. I know I've done nothing to deserve such kindness, but I promise I will do everything I can to repay your generosity."

March rested his hand on Prince Renner's

shoulder and gave it a squeeze. "You can repay us by being happy."

"Hear, hear," Hatter said with approval. "I couldn't have said it better myself. We shall be in touch, Prince Renner. Until then, we wish you a fond farewell and a wonderful rest of your trip here."

After they left, Prince Renner sat down again and surprised me by sprawling on top of the table with a pained groan. "Please tell me I wasn't nearly as embarrassing as I think I was. Because I kind of want to crawl into a hole and die right now."

"You have nothing to be concerned about," I reassured him.

"*I. Pet. March*!" He banged his head against the table. "Why did I do that?"

"Because you felt a strange urge compelling you to do so?"

He turned his head to look at me. "It was like I couldn't control my hand. It *had* to know what his hair felt like. How did you know?"

I grinned at him. "Lucky guess."

"They were *so* nice to me, and I had to ruin it by acting like a weirdo. I bet they already regret offering to help me." Prince Renner sighed heavily. "But it was like every time I looked at March, it felt like an electric shock jolted my heart and my brain got stupid. What's wrong with me?"

I reached over to ruffle his hair. "Absolutely nothing. Now, stop moping, and let's get lunch."

He lifted his head off the table and smiled at me. "I'd like that."

"I'll even tell you some stories about March," I promised with a wink. It would be a fun way to pass the time before I could get Rei alone in his bedroom later.

After facing off with my finance minister, I was officially over people for the day. His opposition to my desire to cut taxes made it tempting to fire him, but I refused to be like my mother and make such rash employment decisions.

I held my breath as I dunked under the water in my bath. When I resurfaced, I startled with a yelp at the sight of Cheshire sitting in front of me in his human form, grinning at me like he always did when he caught me by surprise. I splashed him in the face with water in payback before pushing my hair back from my eyes. "What are you doing here?"

"As you might remember, unlike normal cats, I quite enjoy baths." Cheshire crawled over to me on all fours, his tail waving high in the air with amusement.

He straddled over me, running his hands up my chest to rest on my shoulders as he leaned closer. "I always appreciate having a reason to get you wet, naked, and under me."

Before I could protest, he cupped my face in his hands to give me a sensual kiss, teasing me with his slightly rough tongue. I remembered how startled I had been the first time we kissed, when I felt those unexpectedly soft spines rub against me. Instead of being repulsed, I drew a perverted pleasure from that and his fanged front teeth.

It was glorious being able to pull him against me, to feel his hard length pressing against me, and not have to push him away. I trailed my hands up his back until I buried one in his hair and tugged him closer for a deep taste. Every kiss made me crave a hundred more as I enjoyed indulging in him without having to worry about the consequences for once.

When he drew back, it gave me a moment to breathe. I didn't resist as he repositioned himself behind me. He used his magic to bring a bottle of rose-scented shampoo. I closed my eyes with a hum of contentment as he massaged it in, which made even me want to purr. "It's been a long time since you've groomed me."

He thoroughly worked the shampoo into a lather

as he continued. I expected a smart-aleck reply, so his sincere response surprised me. "I've missed taking care of you like this." His magic formed a small rain cloud that poured water down on my head to wash away the suds. "But if you would not let me into your bed, I knew this level of intimacy would never be accepted."

I pulled my knees up to my chest and wrapped my arms around them. "There aren't enough apologies for the harm I did to us."

He flicked my ear with a playful admonishment. "Naughty king. If you try to ruin bath time with somber regrets, I will have to punish you."

I rubbed the sore spot with a grumble. "That threat is soon to become meaningless. At this point, you have more of my crowns than I do." Stealing them was one of his favorite ways to get payback.

Cheshire's tone was playful as he took care to rinse out all the shampoo. "Then you would be wise not to anger me."

"What do you do with them?" It was something I had been curious about for a long time.

"I hold on to them for safekeeping while I wait for you to come to your senses." He stopped the rain, allowing him to put conditioner in my hair. I closed my eyes as I soaked up the attention. "You only have three left. Once those are mine, I believe I become king since I have all the crowns."

"You would hate everything about being king. It means following all the rules you abhor." I sighed with a heavy weariness from how hard the past three years had been.

"But it would also mean I could make up my own rules. My first rule would be you have to be with me. The second one is that you would have to live a life of happiness." Cheshire started the rain cloud again, which rinsed the conditioner from my hair. "And my third is that you have to love me forever."

"That is what I wish for more than anything," I said in a soft voice. "What will change once we're mates?"

"For one, loving me forever becomes literal. Your soul becomes bound to mine, and since I am an immortal shifter, that means you become an immortal human." He continued rinsing my hair, making sure he rinsed everywhere.

I frowned with concern. "An immortal king? I can't imagine that my people would be thrilled with that."

"If you were a ruler like your mother, that would be true. But you are a kind and just king, so your people will rejoice at the peace and stability your long reign will bring to the Kingdom of Hearts." Cheshire summoned a comb and began running it through my hair. He had enchanted it to be painless by never catching on any knots. "With me at your side, it will hopefully be less onerous since you can share your burden with me."

"It's already better knowing that we can be together without fear." My heart felt lighter than it had since my days as an innocent boy.

"You will also gain an ability that will change our game of hide-and-seek." He sounded more amused than upset.

His comment intrigued me. "What do you mean?"

"Through our bond, you will always be able to sense me and my emotions."

"Meaning I'll be able to tell when you're invisibly lurking nearby?" That was a wonderful perk.

He continued combing my hair. "Yes, you will feel my presence."

Something wasn't adding up. "Why don't you sound upset about me ruining your fun?"

"Because there is also a benefit to you being the only person who is aware I'm there." He started working on a new section of straightening my hair. "I could curl up in your lap to comfort you during a stressful meeting. Or I could pleasure you during a boring one, provided no other shifters were present."

"First of all, you're not allowed to do that—ever—regardless of who is at the meeting. Secondly, why does it matter if it's a meeting with a shifter?"

"Because they can smell me, even if they cannot see me." I could hear the grin in his voice. "And they could easily scent your arousal."

I glanced at him over my shoulder. "Which means Bianco knew how our morning got started today?"

His grin turned naughty. "Yes, but he has no room to judge when he and his mate are as amorous as rabbits in the spring."

"I did *not* need to know that." The thought of Bianco being aware every time Cheshire and I were intimate made me groan. "And I suppose there's nothing I can do to keep our private moments hidden from him?"

"You have nothing to be embarrassed about. Bianco is a good friend and a man of discretion with an insatiable mate. He won't judge." Cheshire draped my hair over my shoulder, baring it so he could trail kisses along it and up my neck. "Besides, as my mate, you should smell like you're mine."

"Before you get too distracted, would you like me

to return the favor of grooming you?" I asked. I knew how important it was to Cheshire as a cat shifter.

He chuckled as he embraced me from behind. "It would be ever so kind of you. I have missed your gentle touch."

We shifted positions. I took my time working the shampoo into his hair, using my nails to scratch his scalp just the way he liked it. His soft purrs of contentment healed something within me that had been broken for far too long after years of denying him everything we both wanted.

The storm cloud turned on once more, helping me wash the shampoo out of his beautiful fuchsia-streaked purple hair. "I'm curious. Have you always enjoyed baths, or did you learn to like them because it meant spending time with me wet and naked while we groomed each other?"

"I didn't mind them before, but you made bath time much more enjoyable." His cat ears twitched on the top of his head as water continued to fall on him. "It's not nearly as much fun by myself—unless I'm thinking about you."

His words brought a blush to my cheeks. "I'm sure you were cursing me for my stubbornness far more than you were having such naughty thoughts about me."

"I can assure you, I *always* have naughty thoughts about you." Cheshire's tail brushed against my prick when I reached for the conditioner to use next. "Besides, the chase reminded me of how I had to pursue you when we first met. It brings back fond memories, not frustration."

"For a cat, you were very dogged in your pursuit of me." I grinned as he purred louder while I rubbed the conditioner into his beautiful hair.

"I had to be. Otherwise, you would have run away from me forever." The little storm cloud rained down on him again to help with the conditioner. I had forgotten how useful it was compared to dunking under the water. "And while I have a lifetime of forever to live, I refuse to spend it without you as part of it."

His words melted my heart. "I feel the same way. Try as hard as I might, I couldn't bear living without you, even when I was forced to try." A thought occurred to me. "Is being your fated mate why it hurt so much to push you away?"

"When our hearts and soul are one, it makes it all the more painful to be apart."

When the rain cloud stopped its downpour, I gently wrung out his hair before I began combing it.

"How did fate decide to pair us together? What is it about me that makes me yours?"

"I know a lot of somethings, nothings, and everythings. It is to be expected of a Cheshire cat as grand as myself. But not even an all-knowing shifter like me can answer why fate made you my perfect mate."

A mock gasp escaped from me as I pretended to be shocked. "You? Not know something? Why, I've never heard such an outlandish thing in all my life."

He snickered at my sarcasm. "You jest, but my all-seeing brother couldn't answer that question. What I can tell you is that from the very moment I first saw you enter that forest glade, my beast could smell that you were *ours*."

I shivered at the dark rumble in his voice that bellied his hidden beast. As much as I adored my playful Chess, I got an exhilarating thrill out of being the center of intense attention of his wilder half. "But what does that smell like?"

The shadows in his voice grew darker as his beast came to the surface. "Like we needed to pin you down and have our wicked way with you to make you *ours*. But *he* wouldn't let us claim what was rightfully ours." It was almost cute hearing his animalistic side pouting about Cheshire's restraint. "We have waited endlessly, and now when you are *finally* willing, we *still* aren't allowed to form our rightful mating bond with our beloved. We grow impatient."

I snorted at that. "When have either of you been patient about anything?"

In a single heartbeat, I was suddenly flat on my back on the floor, with Cheshire's beast pinning me down. His claws dug into my wrists as his amber eyes glowed an unnatural gold. The heat of his arousal pressing against me made me inhale sharply as my prick grew hard with excitement. It had been *so* long since I had tangoed with his wild side. "You dare ask that when we have waited almost fifty years for you?" Cheshire's beast demanded with a growl. "When it has been three painfully celibate years since we have had the pleasure of coming inside you?"

The anger made my heart skip a beat but not from fear. It was with excitement and anticipation because I knew what happened when his other half was pushed to the brink. "Then why haven't you—"

He didn't let me finish my question. It was impossible to do so when he kissed me with an aggression that made me hungry for more, especially when he tugged on my lower lip with his fangs.

I didn't say anything when he kissed his way down my body. The rough drag of his tongue against my nipple while his claws toyed with the other made me moan. I should have been embarrassed at how wanton and needy I sounded, but he hadn't been the only one who had suffered long and lonely nights.

Cheshire's beast slid back into the water, then roughly tugged me forward and spread my legs farther apart. My heart leapt into my chest as he leaned closer to take little licks along the base of my prick. The closer he moved to the tip, the louder I got. My hands found purchase in his hair when he took my hard length into the wet heat of his mouth.

The more he toyed with me, the more I became undone. I writhed underneath him with breathy pleas, completely at his mercy as he used his wicked tongue to drive me wild with lust.

After retracting his claws back into human nails, his magic helped ease his fingers inside me. I clamped my hand over my mouth to smother the shout that wanted to break out from the over-whelming pleasure of it all. To go from nothing to that so quickly was almost more than I could bear.

He stroked me inside, making me yearn for some-thing else entirely. I tried to resist, but his magic pulled my hand away from my face. His beast stopped his fellatio to purr, "No, let us hear you. We have waited a long time for this moment."

When his mouth was on me once again, a

whimper got caught in my throat as he stepped up his efforts. I couldn't get the words out to beg for mercy. But like he always did, Cheshire and his beast knew when I was at my breaking point. He took me down to the base and purred around my length, with the vibrations sending reverberating shivers up my spine.

The exquisite feeling was more than I could bear. I came with a hard gasp. "Chess!"

He swallowed me down, then put on a show of licking me clean while I whimpered from the overload. "Oh, how we've missed your taste," he rumbled in approval. "Almost as much as we miss being buried in your tight heat." His fingers continued pumping into me, making me squirm under him.

Despite having climaxed, my body still moved with his, desperate for more. Pride be damned, I moaned, "Please, Chess! I need—"

"Oh, we know *exactly* what you need," his beast said with a rumbling laugh. He gathered me into his arms and carried me toward the bedroom as I held on to him, like I was a princess instead of a king. "And we will give it to you until your voice is raw from calling out our name."

FIFTEEN

CHESHIRE

I wasn't about to let my beast have all the fun. It took effort to force him back into the shadows where he normally lurked. The battle was worth it when I saw Rei spread out on the bed, his wet hair flared behind him. He was there, just mine for the taking. The urge to disobey Bianco and start forming the mating bond was tempting, but I was a cat of my word. My king had sacrificed so much for his people, and I would not dishonor him in such a way. But it was hard when the combined scent of his lust and satisfaction was intoxicating.

"How angry is your beast that you put him away?" Rei asked.

"He's more irate than a pack of fire buzzbees after someone kicked their nest." I crawled over to Rei to pin him down once more. "But he is not my concern right now. Only you are."

Since my beast had enjoyed a rougher start, I took my time retracing his paths with tender touches and kisses. Rei was putty in my hands as I worshipped him with all the love in my heart. After having to wait so long, it was something I would never take for granted. I would treasure him like the sacred gift he was.

"Please, I don't know how much more I can take," Rei groaned as I moved closer to his renewed erection. He lifted his hips to give me a hint.

That was all I needed to move on. Allowing my magic to slick his channel and stretch him properly, I took enormous pleasure in *finally* pressing inside him at long last. It felt like coming home, making both of us moan as we relearned how to move as one. I lost myself in the gentle rocking of our bodies as I continued to trail my claws against him, raising chills on his fair skin.

He tugged me down for a kiss that begged me for forgiveness, for denying us the pleasure of being made whole. But all the longing had been worth it to feel him embracing me as we fell deeper into each other with every pump of my hips.

Rei wrapped his legs around my waist. I hitched

them higher, earning me a beautiful gasp when combined with the shift in positions. It made it harder to control myself.

Despite my best intentions, I moved with more urgency as I neared my peak. Rei looped his arms over my neck with a plaintive cry that stirred my beast once more. I held my wildness back, but I gave in to my need for a harsher rhythm.

Rei's body kept pace with mine, with both of us moving in perfect sync. My pleasure skyrocketed when his blunt nails dug into my skin as his thighs squeezed me tighter. He became even louder when I used my magic to make my penis swell at the base as the tiny spines, blunted into bumps, grew bigger. The effect had always driven him wild, and judging by the way he arched his back and cried out while riding my cock harder, he was still a fan.

His free abandon was all it took to push me over the edge. I pushed in as deep as I could and came hard with a rumbling growl, thrusting until I was spent. It was only when I paused that I realized Rei had come a second time, making a beautiful mess on his stomach. I was tempted to lap it up.

Before I could, he tugged me down for another kiss. It whispered secrets about all his love and affection for me. Our reunion was everything I had been dreaming about for the past three years. I had finally come home, and Rei was one step closer to being my bonded mate.

O nce I had Rei cleaned up, it was my turn to be cuddled. I sprawled over his chest with a contented purr, which grew louder when he embraced me with one arm while petting my hair with his other hand. It was like the perfect dessert after the best meal of my life.

He was quiet for a long while, which wasn't unusual. After making love, he was often peaceful and at ease, in no rush to think much of anything. It was one of the rare times he could stop all his stress and anxieties from running amok. But he eventually asked, "How is what we just did different from mating?"

"It is what you humans so fondly call 'making love,' I believe," I replied in a teasing tone, my tail waving behind me.

"I'm serious, Chess. What is the difference between the two?"

"Magic."

Rei sighed. "Is there a reason you're dancing around the topic? Will mating hurt or something?"

"No, not at all," I assured him. "My answer was not facetious. Magic makes all the difference."

I could hear the frown in his voice. "But you use your magic on me every time you get me ready for you."

"When you are inside me, it will allow me to merge your magic with mine," I explained.

"*My* magic?" He scoffed. "I'm human. We don't have magic. Alistair was the one exception as the descendant of the original Alice, who carried around all of Wonderland's dark and light magic."

"Wrong. You have latent magic buried deep in the depths of your heart."

Rei's fingers drifted up to toy with my velveteen ears that he loved so much. "Now I know you're messing with me."

"In ancient times, all the human royal families of Wonderland were gifted with magic by the gods as proof of their divine right to rule," I explained.

"Everyone knows that's old folklore used to justify why certain families had the power to rule over others." He was silent for a long moment before a chill ran through him. "If my mother or Rex had been able to use magic, their reign of terror would have been even worse. No one would have survived." As awful as the thought was, he wasn't wrong.

Not wanting him to think about such things, I continued my story. "Over the eons, the magic bestowed upon humans waned, until it was all but forgotten about."

"But how does that happen?"

"You saw how quickly our world forgot about shifters after they all but disappeared when Alice returned home the final time," I reminded him. "Human attention spans are short, and their suspicions are many."

"Are you saying you can feel the magic within me, or are you working off the promises of ancient legends?"

Rather than answer with words, I propped myself up so I could hold my hand over his heart.

He gazed at me skeptically. "What are you doing?"

"You'll see." I used my magic to call out to his. It was deep in slumber, but with some gentle coaxing, it stirred within him. I guided it to unfurl and spark, waiting to catch fire.

Rei pressed his hand over mine against his chest

as he looked at me with wide red eyes. "What is *that*?"

"*That* is your magic." It was still weak and mewling to me like a blind kitten in need of help. As much as I wanted to awaken his magic to its full glory, it was too dangerous to continue. Once I felt it merge with mine, there would be no stopping me or my beast from forming our mating bond with Rei. I withdrew my power for his sake.

He frowned as he moved his hand away. "Where did it go?"

"Back to sleep." I could feel it curling up inside his heart once more, exhausted from its efforts to make itself known for the first time in over one hundred and fifty years. "It's very weak, but it's there, waiting to come to life. And when you are inside me, I will merge my magic with yours to strengthen it. Once you climax inside me, the mating bond will forge between us."

"Shouldn't that be the end if our magic is joined at that point?"

"Not quite." I lay back down on him, making myself comfortable. "My beast will take over and finish binding our souls, which will result in the interwoven rings on our fingers that Bianco and Alistair have. Only then will we share a formal mating bond and can live happily ever after for the rest of time."

He hugged me tighter. "I like the sound of that." He fell silent again before asking, "Wait, will I be able to use magic once our mating bond has formed?"

"Given that Alistair can use magic, I imagine you should, as well."

"But isn't that only because of his connection to the original Alice?"

"I guess we will find out soon." I snuggled against Rei with a contented purr. "Because you're mine tomorrow night, regardless of Bianco's plans. We have waited long enough. As dear a friend as Bianco is, he is testing the limits of what I can endure."

"I'm sure he'll have everything taken care of by then. And if he doesn't, I still won't stop you." Rei guided me up to meet his gaze. "Thank you for not giving up on me."

"I could never give up on you when you are the very thing that makes me live and breathe." Guiding him closer, I claimed a gentle kiss. "You are my beloved, who I love above all others, even when you're being a stubborn cat about things."

His grin was beautiful and free of shadows. "It takes one to know one."

"And that is why we're perfect for each other."

His unrestrained laughter was like the sun returning after a long and cold winter. And tomorrow, he would finally be bonded to me for the rest of our eternal lives. The return of night couldn't come soon enough.

My body ached with a pleasant soreness the next day, a wonderful reminder of how Cheshire and I had spent the evening relearning each other's bodies. The small taste had left me hungry for more, making me act with a rashness I normally avoided. I craved him, and I would not be denied, schedule be damned. Bianco would eventually forgive me.

After lunch, I returned to my tower, locking the door behind me. Thankfully, Cheshire didn't disappoint me. He was already waiting for me in my bedroom with his trademark grin. "I'm amazed you only lasted half the day before you came back to me." With a small gesture of his hand, he removed all of our clothing. Seeing him hard and wanting spiked my arousal higher. "I figured you were stubborn enough to hold out until after dinner."

"I'm tired of waiting." I closed the distance between us, tugging him down for a demanding kiss. It fueled the fire raging inside me, making me burn even brighter from my desperate need for Cheshire. "Get on the bed."

"Yes, Your Majesty," Cheshire replied in a cheeky tone. He pounced on the bed before rolling onto his back and holding his arms open to me. It was the best kind of heaven to accept his embrace without having to fight anymore.

My reward was a teasing kiss that confirmed I had made the right decision to skip my meeting with the postmaster about what portrait illustration of me should be used for next year's new stamps. I could keep kissing Cheshire forever, but I craved more.

Despite my impatience, I enjoyed relearning Cheshire's body as I explored him with my lips and fingertips. Slowly making my way downward, I took great pleasure in stroking his cock, which felt so different from my own because of the soft bumps at the base. I appreciated he always used his magic to make sure he never extended the spines to their full length since that would hurt me. But the sweet spot of having those gentle bumped ridges drove me wild in a way a human penis couldn't. It was yet another benefit of having a magical shifter as a partner.

"So, how naughty are we going to be?" Cheshire asked. "Are we simply going to indulge in some afternoon delight, or are you ready to say the hell with Bianco's planning and form a mating bond?" His tail waved on the bed. "I know which choice I'm voting for."

After spending the past three years denying myself everything I wanted, it was a simple decision to make. "Tell me what to do."

"All I need is for you to be inside me, and I can handle the rest. I'm slicked and ready for you." It was amazing having a partner who could prepare themselves with magic.

I repositioned myself over him, lifting his hips as I guided my prick into him. The tight heat of his channel embracing me so tightly made me gasp as I sank deeper into him.

Once I was fully sheathed, Cheshire's magic washed over me. I closed my eyes as I experienced that strange flutter in my heart from the previous night. The sensation stirred before it flared with a heat that sent fire through my veins as it lit me up inside. It gave me a power rush I had never felt before, making me headier than when I was sitting next to Vivalter at one of Hatter's tea parties.

My body moved on instinct, sending me to dizzying new heights as I felt the echoes of Cheshire's pleasure in my heart from our tentative connection. It made me want to crawl into his magical soul and stay there forever in its warm embrace. Every thrust of my hips sent me flying higher, and the only thing keeping me grounded was Cheshire's hands caressing me all over.

I had so many things I wanted to tell him, but I couldn't find the words as I fell deeper into our connection. The echoing pleasure was unlike anything I had ever experienced before, and it made me greedy for more. The experience was even more enjoyable when Cheshire's powers penetrated me to prepare for the next part. On instinct, I leaned forward and kissed him. I could feel the magic moving between us take root in my heart.

White heat flooded through me, pushing me to the very brink of climax. I didn't want it to be over too soon, but I couldn't make myself slow down as my body acted on its own accord. There was a driving need demanding more of Cheshire and the feelings between us. "I love you so much, Chess," I murmured, finding the words to say what I had always felt.

"As much as I love you."

I pushed in as deep as I could before I came with a soft cry. An explosion of ecstasy detonated inside of me, which was amplified by our souls forming the initial link. It was such an intense rush of feelings that I lost sight of myself in the chaos of it all. The only thing I was sure of was that Cheshire was with me, and I loved him more than life itself. As long as he was mine, life was worth living.

While I was floating so high, I barely noticed that he guided me onto my hands and knees. But my heart skipped a beat since my body still remembered that position meant Cheshire's beast was coming out to play. And oh, what fun it was when he did.

The formation of the mating bond was incredible. I basked in the beauty of being able to feel Rei on a new level, but my beast was impatient to finish the ritual before someone came to interrupt. It was a concern I shared, which was why I took action instead of simply enjoying the nascent bond.

My beast clamored for control, but I refused to miss out on all the fun. To appease him, I guided Rei onto his hands and knees. My magic had already readied him, so I didn't wait to push into his welcoming heat. Rei's protracted moan of relief from being filled made my beast urge me to move. I had no desire to resist.

Holding Rei's hips, I took great pleasure in how

our bodies perfectly fit together as we moved in perfect sync. The bond strengthened with every movement. I was like a man possessed as my beast attempted to wrest control away from me.

Not wanting to miss a thing, I offered my beast a rare chance at unifying our consciousness so we could both enjoy the moment. To my great surprise, he eagerly agreed. As we merged, our combined powers flared, which allowed us to form an even stronger bond with Rei's fledgling magic that had blossomed so beautifully in his heart.

With my beast's instincts at the forefront, our actions became rougher, more animalistic as we rutted against our mate with fervent need. Our claws sank into his soft skin, but we were still careful not to draw blood. His complete surrender drove us to cover Rei's body with ours, allowing us to sink our teeth into his neck to hold him in place while our pace got rougher. Rei's cry of pleasure was so beautiful it made us redouble our efforts.

Everything was a white heat in our mind as we chased after the mating bond. The hard pace was too much to maintain for long. Since we knew Rei derived so much enjoyment from it, we used magic to make the nubbed base of our cock expand inside him. It made him push harder against us with a shout of ecstasy as we sank our fangs deeper into his tender flesh.

When he tightened his channel around us, we pushed in to the hilt and came with a feral growl. As our seed marked him as ours, the second part of the mating bond took hold. It entwined the tentative connection to create an unbreakable bond with the one we would love for the rest of time.

The first gift it blessed us with was Rei's orgasm echoing through our connection, allowing us to feel it as if it were our own. He collapsed to the bed with a protracted moan of satisfaction, making us preen with pride that we had pleasured our mate so thoroughly.

Our seed leaked out of him when we pulled out, making us purr at seeing him intimately marked as ours. It made us wish to push him to his limits, but the mating bond's formation and two intense rounds had left us drained.

We curled around Rei, savoring our new connection that allowed us to feel him so deeply. Even after he drifted to sleep, we lingered in wakefulness a little longer to enjoy our closeness. Bringing our hand up, the interwoven band of red and purple from our souls wrapped around our ring finger, the physical proof we had successfully mated. It made us rumble with deep joy. Now, no one could ever take him from us again.

When I awoke, my beast had retreated to recover from the exhaustion of using so much magic to form the bond. It took a moment to realize what had stirred me. I could feel Rei using his newly gained powers to prod our connection with curiosity.

I sat up with a yawn. "Yes?"

"Sorry, did I wake you?" Rei asked in a remorseful voice.

"You did, but that's not a bad thing." I ran my fingers through my hair. "How does the bond feel to you?"

He hummed with happiness. "I've never felt more loved in my life. But it is strange to feel you inside me."

"That's because you will always carry a part of my heart within you." I touched the anchor of our bond within him, making him shiver. "Now, you can never be alone because I'm forever with you."

Joy reverberated through our new connection. "I

don't think I've ever been this happy in my life. It's like I'm a new man."

"How does the rest of you feel? We weren't too rough, were we?" My beast always tried to be respectful, but sometimes his wildness could get a little out of hand.

"No, everything was perfect. Everything *is* perfect." Rei stretched with a moan. "It makes me want to run away for a bit, so it can stay that way a little longer before some problem inevitably comes up that takes me out of this beautiful bubble we're in right now."

"Your wish is my command." I gathered him in my arms and teleported us to the one place where the world had never been able to reach us, out by the waterfall at the old palace ruins.

Rei blinked rapidly as he took in his surroundings. "Wait, what just happened?"

"Can you think of a better place to escape to than here?" I gestured at the surrounding emptiness. The only witnesses to us were the thicket of woods, the birds flying overhead, and the thunderous waterfall pouring into the beautiful blue lagoon.

"This is the real place? We're not actually at the palace?"

I took his hand and led him into the warm water.

When he didn't follow me, I swam under the water before popping up farther into the lagoon. "We're really here. There is nowhere in Wonderland I can't bring us now that we're bonded."

He swam over to me, running his fingers through his wet hair when he stood up straight once more. "Then why did we always have to take the long walk here before?"

I wrapped my legs around his waist as I looped my arms over his neck. "So we didn't miss all the fun adventures along the way." My heart skipped a beat when he cupped my ass and gave it a squeeze.

He rested his forehead against mine with a chuckle. "You never cease to amaze me."

"Shall we play our favorite game of tag, you're mine?" I pushed off him and put some distance between us. "Winner takes loser."

Excitement sparked in our bond when Rei's expression turned predatory. "Game on." He lunged at me, but I dodged his grasp.

I moved deeper into the lagoon, with Rei hot on my tail. He made another pass for me, but I shifted into my cat form to get away.

"Hey! That's cheating!" Rei protested with a laugh.

I paddled away from him with a grin. "You can't catch me, regardless of what form I take."

He made another grab for me, almost catching my tail. I shifted into my smaller kitten form, luring him closer under the guise of my little legs frantically trying to paddle away from him. When he grabbed for me, I dunked under the water and shifted into my human form, allowing me to pop up behind him and pull him to my chest. "Got you!"

He struggled in my arms. "That's cheating, and you know it!"

His protest made me snicker. "I still won."

"Best two out of three," he demanded. "I'll race you to the other side of the waterfall."

Before I could agree, he dove under the water. I gave chase, but he pulled ahead of me. Since he was a strong swimmer, I had to resort to something more clever. I gave myself a mermaid tail and used the fin to get an edge on him. I made it by a whisker, sitting on the edge of the lagoon a mere second before he popped up from underwater.

He splashed me in annoyance when he saw I bested him. "How did you beat me?"

I waved my shimmering purple-and-pink mermaid tail at him with a cheeky grin. "Did you really think a human could defeat a catfish?"

His incredulous protest was adorable. As he swam closer, his expression shifted to awe. He ran his hands up my mermaid tail to where it blended into my human top half. "I want to be mad at you for cheating, but you're too beautiful this way. You look like the handsome mermen in the fairy tales I used to read when I was a boy."

I could feel his arousal through our bond. "I imagine you would have a great deal more fun with that fantasy now that you're a man."

He continued idly stroking my tail. "And what are you suggesting?"

"Since I won best two out of three through under-handed means, perhaps we can have a compromise." I allowed my erection to emerge from a slit, earning a sharp inhale from Rei. "If you ride me, it's still tech-nically winner takes loser, but you're coming out on top. That way, we both win."

When he didn't respond, I used my magic to prep him. He scowled at me. "It's a testament to how much you've corrupted me that I'm actually tempted by such a ridiculous proposition."

I hopped back into the water, resting my arms behind me on the rocky edge. It allowed me to float on my back, with my erection standing proudly. "You know you want to pretend you're a shipwrecked king who falls in love with the amorous merman who saved your life."

"You did save my life." Rei moved in close enough to kiss me, making our bond flare to life. I helped ease him onto my arousal, using my mermaid tail to keep us afloat.

It took a few tries before Rei found a rhythm that worked for him. He braced himself on my stomach as I enjoyed flicking my fin to propel my thrusts into him on his downward bounces. The sound of our bodies connecting heightened my pleasure, as did feeling the water lapping with our vigorous movements.

Our mating bond sang as Rei rode me hard. I helped him keep balance by holding on to his glorious royal ass to guide his movements. I used my magic to stroke his prick, making him tilt his head with a moan. He arched his back and came with a soft cry of "Chess!"

I gave him a moment to enjoy the ecstasy before I reversed our positions, then guided him to brace his back against the rocky edge of the waterfall entrance. When he wrapped his legs around my waist, it allowed me to use my tail to its full benefit of force-fully driving my cock into him with every flip of my fin. Rei's cries of pleasure spurred me on as I pumped hard and fast before climaxing inside him. "Rei!"

He hugged me closer when I finished, giving me a passionate kiss that made our mating bond burn brightly between us with overwhelming love and affection.

We'd eventually have to return to the palace, but behind the waterfall, we were still in a world of our own, where no one could reach us.

After having our fun, I created a makeshift bed under the shady trees for Rei to rest. He deserved a good catnap after our vigorous lovemaking earlier. I was curled up in my feline form on his stomach, soaking up our private time away from the stress of the world.

A rainbow butterfly fluttering into the clearing disturbed our peace. I narrowed my eyes at Vivalter's arrival.

He landed on a nearby flower, letting his wings flutter as he settled. His voice was barely louder than a whisper in his animal form. "There is no need to glare at me, dear brother."

"This is *our* place." It was the one spot in all of Wonderland for only us.

"And so it shall remain. I am merely passing through to congratulate you on your successful mating bond. It is a most frabjous occasion."

I regarded him with suspicion. "You haven't come to warn me that some great peril is about to befall us because I was selfish and didn't wait for Bianco to give us permission?"

"Your union is a blessed one, approved by fate itself. With a bond as strong as yours, you have nothing to fear. I am happy for you, baby brother. And a little envious if I am being truthful."

It was shocking to hear Vivalter admit that. "Then why don't you mate with Hatter?"

Vivalter's antenna twitched in the wind. "That situation has grown more complicated."

I rested my chin on my paws. "The only one complicating things is you."

"No, this is different." Vivalter's wings fluttered in agitation. "Something has happened that I can't explain."

"You'll have to try if you want me to be of any use to you."

"Hatter's time has stopped."

Maybe it was all the lovemaking, but the simple sentence didn't make sense to me. "How?"

"If I knew, I would not be so concerned." His wings flapped once more with unrest. "But when I try to see visions of him in the future, it is as if everything is frozen again, like when he was trapped in the former Queen of Heart's endless tea party. However, he isn't stuck in a time loop again. It defies logic."

"Have you tried asking him about it?"

Vivalter's antenna bobbed. "If I don't have an answer, he certainly will not."

"That's a rather presumptuous assumption." I ignored the haughty tilt of my brother's head. "What about your future?"

"What about it?"

"Hatter's future has always been tied to yours. But if time has stopped his future, has it also stopped yours?"

Vivalter rubbed his front legs together. "I did not think to check." I could hear how that admission pained him. He was silent for a few more moments as he pondered the issue. "Very well. I am off to investigate. Fare thee well, dear brother. We will speak soon. Give my fondest regards to our king."

I waved goodbye with my tail as Vivalter flew away.

It startled me when Rei reached up to give my scruff a good scratch. His voice was drowsy as he asked, "Was that your brother?"

"He wished to congratulate us on his way to solving another world crisis." I lifted my head to meet Rei's gaze. "Apparently, Hatter's time has stopped. Whatever *that* means."

"Like when my mother had him trapped in that sadistic tea party by Father Time?"

That was the last thing I wanted my beloved to think about now. "No, this is something else entirely. But my brother refuses to ask Hatter what could cause such an issue, so it is not our problem to solve." I distracted Rei by kneading his stomach with my front paws.

He chuckled as he gave me an affectionate head rub. "You're such a good little baker," he teased me since he always joked I was making biscuits whenever I did that. "I don't suppose you could summon some food while you're at it? I'm ravished."

"No, you're ravishing. That is quite another thing entirely," I retorted. With a wave of my hand, a basket appeared that was full of the best picnic treats the royal kitchen offered. "After lunch, we can go for another swim."

There was a playful gleam in his eyes. "Only if you promise me a rematch."

"I can deny you nothing. And if you're *really* lucky, you might have another merman sighting." I winked at him, making him laugh as we took the food from the basket.

Seeing him so light and free of the shadows that had plagued him during our time apart meant everything to me. I lived to make my mate happy and would do everything in my magical power to make ours the happiest happily ever after ever.

T wasn't in any rush to return to the palace. In the glade by the lagoon, it felt like Cheshire and I had entered a world where time had stopped, and we were the only two people in all of Wonderland. There would undoubtedly be consequences for our selfishness of escaping without Bianco's explicit consent, but I felt too good to care.

Cheshire nuzzled against my cheek in his cat form. "It is wonderful to feel you so content, mate."

I hugged him to my chest. "It's a happiness I never thought I'd be allowed to have." It was amazing feeling Cheshire and his affection through our bond. "No matter what happens later—"

He booped me on the nose with his paw to inter-

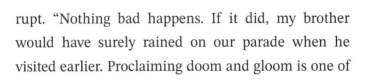

rupt. "Nothing bad happens. If it did, my brother would have surely rained on our parade when he visited earlier. Proclaiming doom and gloom is one of his favorite hobbies, after all."

I was overly familiar with how often Vivalter made dire predictions about the consequences of my actions. "It's surreal that we're allowed to just be happy after everything we've been through. I keep expecting there to be some catch."

"Fate made us mates, and fate always takes care of its own." Cheshire's tail swished over my stomach. "The hard times are behind us now. All we have to do is live happily ever after."

"Bianco and Alistair living in bliss is certainly proof of that." I sighed as I continued petting Cheshire.

"After everything we've been through, it's our turn to be happy forever." Cheshire shifted into his human form, pinning me down as he gave me a hungry kiss that had my prick's full attention. "And our chance to make up for lost time."

I expected him to take me again, which was why it came as such a surprise for him to slide onto my rigid length. His claws dug into my sides as he set a fast and bouncy rhythm. It was a rare treat to enjoy him from that position, so I savored the moment. I cupped his ass in my hands as I helped guide his rough movements, pushing deeper into him every time our bodies met.

As I watched him riding me hard, I couldn't help but marvel at him. "You're so beautiful." I squeezed his ass, earning a rumbling purr of approval. "How did I get lucky enough that you're mine?"

"I could ask you the same thing," he replied with laughter in his tone. He tossed his head back with a sigh of pleasure as his pace grew rougher. "There are few sights more beautiful in this world than you lying under me in ecstasy."

Now that we had a mating bond, it created a magical loop where not only was I making love to him, but I could also feel what he did as I thrust into him. Giving and taking pleasure at the same time in such a new way was beyond anything I had experienced before. It made it hard to last for long. I held out as long as I could before I pulled his body flush with mine so I could come inside him with a gasp. "Chess!"

His orgasm was triggered almost simultaneously, reverberating through me. As he leaned down and kissed me, I happily drowned in his affection. Our happiness had been hard fought but finally won.

Eventually, we would have to return home, but it couldn't hurt to indulge in our love for a little longer.

We had only been back at the palace for a few minutes before there was a knock on the bedroom door. I sighed at the reminder of real life encroaching on what was easily the best day of my life. "Yes?"

A servant called out from the other side. "Master Bianco and Master Alistair wish to know if you are free to meet with them and Prince Renner?"

Cheshire wrapped his arms around me in a warm embrace. "You can always tell them no."

"No, Bianco deserves to know so he can make accommodations for our selfishness." I addressed the servant on the other side of the door. "Have them meet us in my living quarters within the hour."

"Yes, Your Majesty."

The delay gave us enough time to make ourselves presentable and sit on the couch. In true cat fashion, Cheshire proudly sat on my lap in his human form.

"I'm not the royal throne," I dryly reminded him, nudging him to make him sit at my side.

He wouldn't budge. "No, but you're quite comfortable. I think I shall stay."

Before I could belabor the point, Bianco, Alistair, and Prince Renner entered the room with bows. Cheshire waved at them in return as I tilted my head in acknowledgment.

"A hearty congratulations to you on your mating bond," Bianco said with a warm smile as he sat on the couch at my side.

"You're not mad?" Cheshire asked in surprise.

The white rabbit shifter shook his head. "No, nor am I surprised. I am sincerely delighted for you both. It has been a long time coming."

Cheshire pouted. "I wanted you to be at least a *little* mad at me for disobeying."

"I finished with all the preparations yesterday, but I knew you would enjoy yourself more if you thought you were breaking the rules."

That turned Cheshire's frown into a broad grin. "You know me far too well, old friend."

Alistair took a cue from my naughty shifter by sitting in Bianco's lap. "I'm so happy for you!"

"As am I," Prince Renner said as he sat in an oversized red chair.

"Vivalter prophesied that Prince Renner would bring you love, and he was right yet again," Bianco said as he wrapped his arms around his mate and rested his chin on his mate's shoulder. "Everything worked out exactly as it should."

Cheshire shook his head. "Almost everything. Prince Renner still has quite the journey to go on before he finds his beloved. But I am quite certain it will be fantastical fun."

The prince rubbed the back of his head with a nervous laugh. "Provided I don't screw it up and unintentionally cause all-out warfare."

"You have nothing to fear. Not only will you have the help of the famous Cheshire cat, but Hatter and March as well," my mate told him. "We will take good care of you, rest assured."

"I know I must go back, but I'm already dreading it. Staying here these past few days has been the best time of my life. The thought of returning to my parents' awful palace and living under their draconian rules is stifling."

My heart went out to the young royal. Those awful days under my mother's reign of terror were not so far in my past that I could easily forget. "Whenever it becomes too much to bear, remember you will always have sanctuary in my kingdom and here in the palace."

"That means a lot, but something tells me it

wouldn't go well for anyone if my parents thought you were harboring me as a fugitive here." Prince Renner sighed. "It's most unfortunate because your comfortable accommodations here have already spoiled me."

"Once you are settled with March, we will see to it that you have the finest bed," Cheshire promised, causing me to arch my eyebrows in surprise. "You won't have to sleep like you're in the army barracks anymore."

"Thank you for giving me something to look forward to." Prince Renner gestured at Cheshire's hand. "What's that?"

He rubbed his thumb over his ring finger. "It's visual proof of our mating bond. His red soul is entwined with my purple one for the rest of time."

"Ours are blue and pink," Alistair added. "I don't know what makes my soul blue, but I think it's pretty cool."

"Unless I end up lucky enough to have a fated mate, I guess I'll never know what shade my soul is." Prince Renner shrugged to himself. "I wonder how a color is chosen?"

"It's based on your aura," Bianco explained, which was news to me. "Vivalter is the only seer who might be able to tell you without the need for a bond."

"But why ruin the surprise?"

Bianco's lips turned up in a grin. "Speaking of surprises."

Cheshire's tail waved. "Is it a good surprise or a bad surprise?"

"Now that you have formed your mating bond, there is the matter of your official marriage."

I held in a groan. "Are you telling me we have to go through a traditional wedding ceremony?" There were few things that I found less appealing than that.

The white rabbit shifter nodded. "Seeing as it is the only royal wedding you will ever have because of your eternal bond with Cheshire, your people deserve the chance to celebrate with you."

Although the thought of going through such a proper ceremony made me want to run away, he was right. I owed it to my citizens to let them rejoice in my new consort. Cheshire and our union deserved to be celebrated. "When will the ceremony be?"

"Not for several months," Bianco replied, giving me a sigh of relief. "It's not something that we can just throw together, so it will take time to have the event planner arrange such a massive celebration."

"Don't worry. I promise I will be the perfect, charming consort on his absolute best behavior."

Cheshire nuzzled against me, so I gave him a hug. "At least you won't have to go through it alone."

I would never have to go through anything alone ever again. It was the best feeling in the world knowing that no matter what life threw at me, Cheshire would always be grinning at my side, his heart full of love for me. That made me the luckiest man in all of Wonderland.

EPILOGUE

CHESHIRE

LATER THAT NIGHT

Since Rei was in such a good mood, I talked him into going to the top of his tower for some stargazing. It had been such a long time since we had lain on his lounges with nothing to do other than be near each other. "The stars are almost as beautiful as you."

He chuckled as he took my hand in his and gave it a squeeze. "I could say the same to you." He sighed as he looked up at the twinkling night sky. "I can't believe we're allowed to be happy now. It almost doesn't seem real."

"It's as real as my never-ending love for you." I

flooded our bond with all the affection I held for him in my heart so he would know how much I adored him.

"I couldn't be the person he needed, but I hope that Prince Renner is lucky enough to find this kind of happiness with someone." Rei tilted his head to glance over at me. "He deserves to be treasured. It pains me to send him back home, knowing what awaits him."

With everything that had happened, I realized I had never updated my mate about Prince Renner's fate. "You needn't worry about the young princeling. His future will be as happy as ours."

"What makes you say that?"

"Between us, it is because March is his fated mate. I'm delighted by that outcome. I couldn't think of a better partner for the youngling."

Rei's eyes widened in surprise. "Really?"

"Yes, March was caught quite off guard." I chuckled as I remembered his unsettled reaction. "I suspect he will try to resist his beast's urges because he is a consummate gentleman, but I don't foresee him being able to hold back from Prince Renner for very long."

Rei smiled as he looked up at the sky. "That is

actually a relief to hear. March is a good man, who will take care of Prince Renner. Perhaps I needn't worry so much now."

"I'd be happy to distract you," I purred as I straddled him. "It's been a long time since we've made love under the stars."

It was the best kind of bliss when I felt Rei's adoration for me thrumming through our bond as he tugged me down for a kiss. Waiting had been hell, but finally getting to be with the greatest love of my life had been worth every moment apart. We had the rest of eternity to spend together, and I intended to treasure every step of our journey through our eternal life.

Curious if King Rei can reclaim his missing crowns from Cheshire? **Claim your copy of Crowning Achievement today!**

Want to see Prince Renner and March find their happily ever after together? **Read Renner in**

Mirrorland to enjoy their adventurous royal romance.

In the mood for something a little different? **Check out Come from Behind today for an unexpected meet-cute that leads to true love.**

THANK YOU

Thank you for reading **Cheshire in Heartsland**.
Reviews are crucial for helping other readers discover
new books to enjoy. If you want to share your love for
Cheshire and King Rei, please leave a review. I'd
really appreciate it!

Recommending my work to others is also a huge
help. Don't hesitate to give this book a shout-out in
your favorite book rec group to spread the word.

NEXT IN SERIES

AVAILABLE NOW

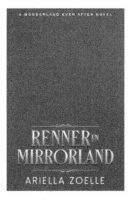

Prince Renner has always dreamed of a life of adventure. Will he find true love with March along the way?

If you love sweetheart shifters, fated mates, first times, and royal romances, **read Renner in Mirror-land today by using the QR code below**!

ACKNOWLEDGMENTS

Cheshire and King Rei's story is something I've been eager to share with everyone! *Alice in Wonderland* was one of my favorite books as a kid because the possibility of living in a world with talking cats was my idea of heaven.

Special thanks goes out to my amazing team of beta readers of Amy Mitchell, Raquel Riley, Lindsay Porter, Tammy Jones, Lisa Klein, Kylie Anderson, Cilla May, Dylan Pope, Jennifer Sharon, Missy Kretschmer, and Ashley Krystalf! I'm so lucky to call these lovely people my friends.

I'm incredibly appreciative of the kind generosity shown to me by Shelia Kilgore, Tammy Jones, Gabriela, Kira, and my other Ko-fi supporters who helped make it possible for me to continue being a full-time author.

I also want to thank everyone who recommends my books in Facebook rec threads. It means everything to me that you share my books with other readers. I'm also filled with endless gratitude to all of my

ARC readers for taking the time to leave such thoughtful reviews.

Pam, Sandra, and Natasha are my dream team and I'm so honored and lucky to work with them.

I can't wait to meet again in **Renner in Mirrorland** and **Come from Behind**!

ABOUT THE AUTHOR

ariella zoelle

WWW.ARIELLAZOELLE.COM

Ariella Zoelle adores steamy, funny, swoony romances where couples are allowed to just be happy. She writes low angst stories full of heat, humor, and heart. But sometimes she's in the mood for something with a bit more angst and drama. If you are too, check out her A.F. Zoelle books.

Get a bonus chapter by using the QR code below!

Made in the USA
Monee, IL
05 February 2023

27130354R00122